Walt Disney's Donald Duck

• A Double Dose of Triple Trouble •

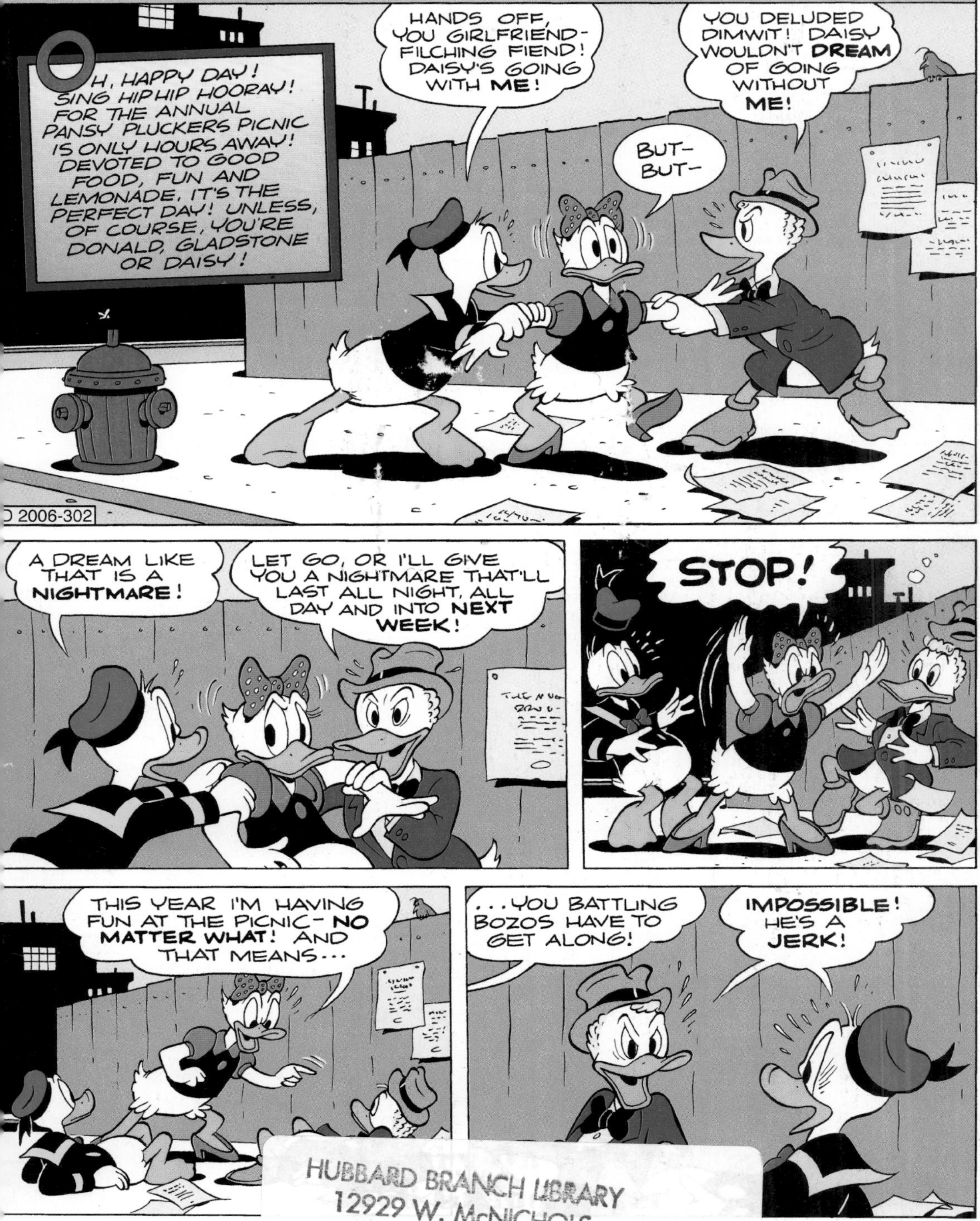
OH, HAPPY DAY! SING HIPHIP HOORAY! FOR THE ANNUAL PANSY PLUCKERS PICNIC IS ONLY HOURS AWAY! DEVOTED TO GOOD FOOD, FUN AND LEMONADE, IT'S THE PERFECT DAY! UNLESS, OF COURSE, YOU'RE DONALD, GLADSTONE OR DAISY!
HANDS OFF, YOU GIRLFRIEND-FILCHING FIEND! DAISY'S GOING WITH **ME**!
YOU DELUDED DIMWIT! DAISY WOULDN'T **DREAM** OF GOING WITHOUT **ME**!
BUT-BUT-
2006-302
A DREAM LIKE THAT IS A **NIGHTMARE**!
LET GO, OR I'LL GIVE YOU A NIGHTMARE THAT'LL LAST ALL NIGHT, ALL DAY AND INTO **NEXT WEEK**!
STOP!
THIS YEAR I'M HAVING FUN AT THE PICNIC- **NO MATTER WHAT!** AND THAT MEANS...
...YOU BATTLING BOZOS HAVE TO GET ALONG!
IMPOSSIBLE! HE'S A **JERK**!

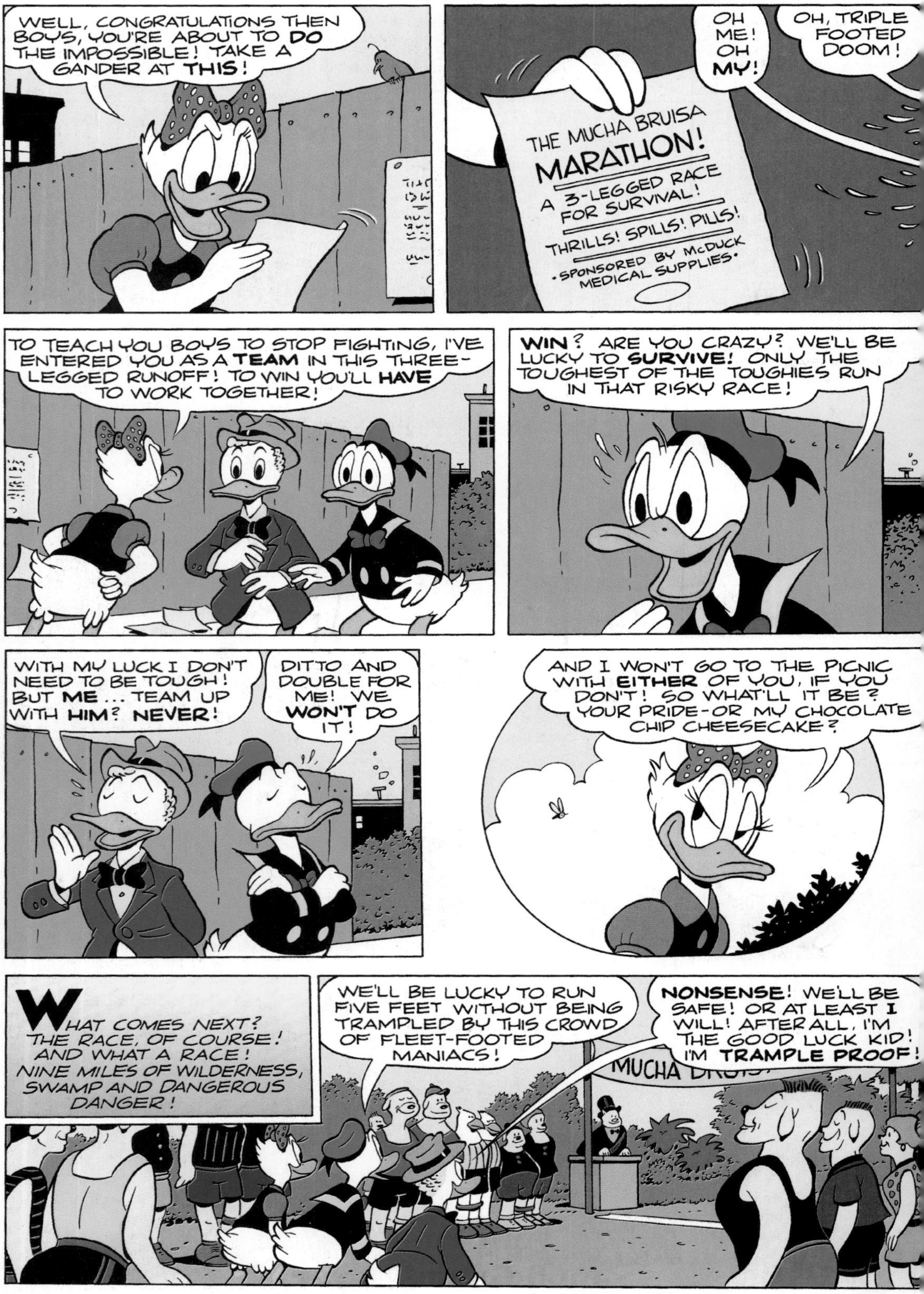
WELL, CONGRATULATIONS THEN BOYS, YOU'RE ABOUT TO DO THE IMPOSSIBLE! TAKE A GANDER AT THIS!
OH ME! OH MY!
OH, TRIPLE FOOTED DOOM!
THE MUCHA BRUISA MARATHON! A 3-LEGGED RACE FOR SURVIVAL! THRILLS! SPILLS! PILLS! •SPONSORED BY McDUCK MEDICAL SUPPLIES•
TO TEACH YOU BOYS TO STOP FIGHTING, I'VE ENTERED YOU AS A TEAM IN THIS THREE-LEGGED RUNOFF! TO WIN YOU'LL HAVE TO WORK TOGETHER!
WIN? ARE YOU CRAZY? WE'LL BE LUCKY TO SURVIVE! ONLY THE TOUGHEST OF THE TOUGHIES RUN IN THAT RISKY RACE!
WITH MY LUCK I DON'T NEED TO BE TOUGH! BUT ME... TEAM UP WITH HIM? NEVER!
DITTO AND DOUBLE FOR ME! WE WON'T DO IT!
AND I WON'T GO TO THE PICNIC WITH EITHER OF YOU, IF YOU DON'T! SO WHAT'LL IT BE? YOUR PRIDE-OR MY CHOCOLATE CHIP CHEESECAKE?
WHAT COMES NEXT? THE RACE, OF COURSE! AND WHAT A RACE! NINE MILES OF WILDERNESS, SWAMP AND DANGEROUS DANGER!
WE'LL BE LUCKY TO RUN FIVE FEET WITHOUT BEING TRAMPLED BY THIS CROWD OF FLEET-FOOTED MANIACS!
NONSENSE! WE'LL BE SAFE! OR AT LEAST I WILL! AFTER ALL, I'M THE GOOD LUCK KID! I'M TRAMPLE PROOF!

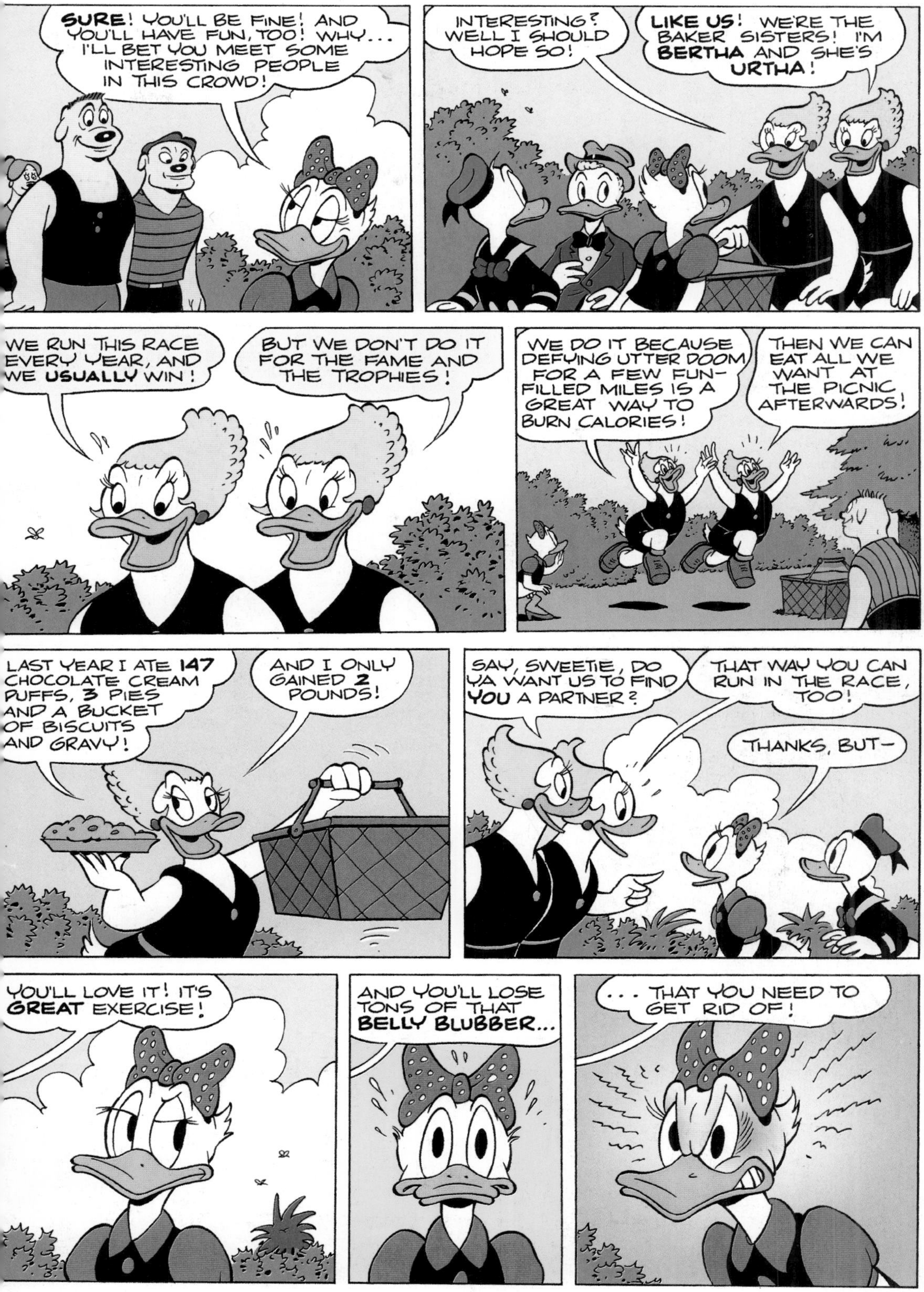
SURE! YOU'LL BE FINE! AND YOU'LL HAVE FUN, TOO! WHY... I'LL BET YOU MEET SOME INTERESTING PEOPLE IN THIS CROWD!
INTERESTING? WELL I SHOULD HOPE SO!
LIKE US! WE'RE THE BAKER SISTERS! I'M BERTHA AND SHE'S URTHA!
WE RUN THIS RACE EVERY YEAR, AND WE USUALLY WIN!
BUT WE DON'T DO IT FOR THE FAME AND THE TROPHIES!
WE DO IT BECAUSE DEFYING UTTER DOOM FOR A FEW FUN-FILLED MILES IS A GREAT WAY TO BURN CALORIES!
THEN WE CAN EAT ALL WE WANT AT THE PICNIC AFTERWARDS!
LAST YEAR I ATE 147 CHOCOLATE CREAM PUFFS, 3 PIES AND A BUCKET OF BISCUITS AND GRAVY!
AND I ONLY GAINED 2 POUNDS!
SAY, SWEETIE, DO YA WANT US TO FIND YOU A PARTNER?
THAT WAY YOU CAN RUN IN THE RACE, TOO!
THANKS, BUT–
YOU'LL LOVE IT! IT'S GREAT EXERCISE!
AND YOU'LL LOSE TONS OF THAT BELLY BLUBBER...
... THAT YOU NEED TO GET RID OF!

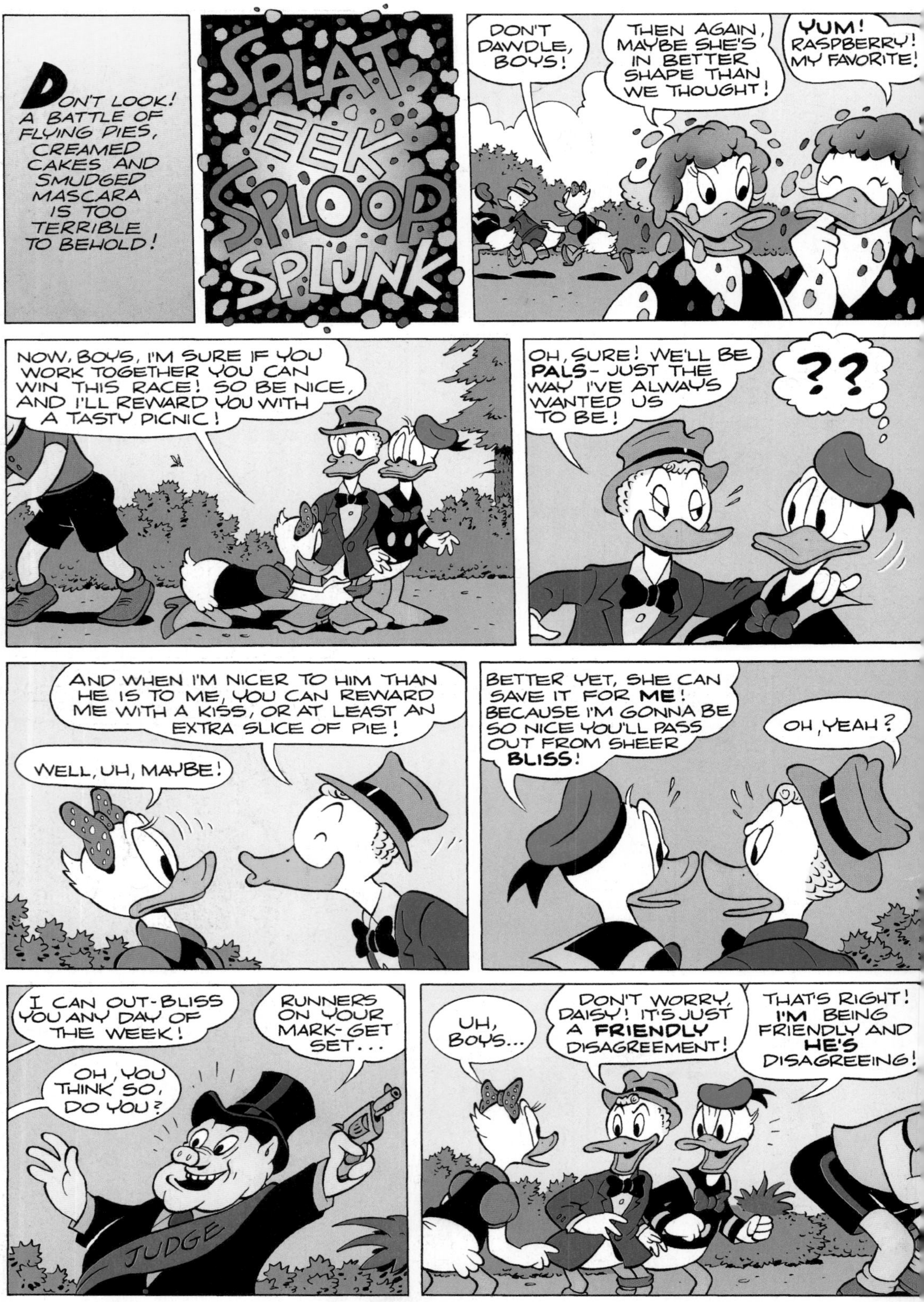
DON'T LOOK! A BATTLE OF FLYING PIES, CREAMED CAKES AND SMUDGED MASCARA IS TOO TERRIBLE TO BEHOLD!
SPLAT
EEK
SPLOOP
SPLUNK
DON'T DAWDLE, BOYS!
THEN AGAIN, MAYBE SHE'S IN BETTER SHAPE THAN WE THOUGHT!
YUM! RASPBERRY! MY FAVORITE!
NOW, BOYS, I'M SURE IF YOU WORK TOGETHER YOU CAN WIN THIS RACE! SO BE NICE, AND I'LL REWARD YOU WITH A TASTY PICNIC!
OH, SURE! WE'LL BE PALS- JUST THE WAY I'VE ALWAYS WANTED US TO BE!
??
AND WHEN I'M NICER TO HIM THAN HE IS TO ME, YOU CAN REWARD ME WITH A KISS, OR AT LEAST AN EXTRA SLICE OF PIE!
WELL, UH, MAYBE!
BETTER YET, SHE CAN SAVE IT FOR ME! BECAUSE I'M GONNA BE SO NICE YOU'LL PASS OUT FROM SHEER BLISS!
OH, YEAH?
I CAN OUT-BLISS YOU ANY DAY OF THE WEEK!
OH, YOU THINK SO, DO YOU?
RUNNERS ON YOUR MARK- GET SET...
JUDGE
UH, BOYS...
DON'T WORRY, DAISY! IT'S JUST A FRIENDLY DISAGREEMENT!
THAT'S RIGHT! I'M BEING FRIENDLY AND HE'S DISAGREEING!

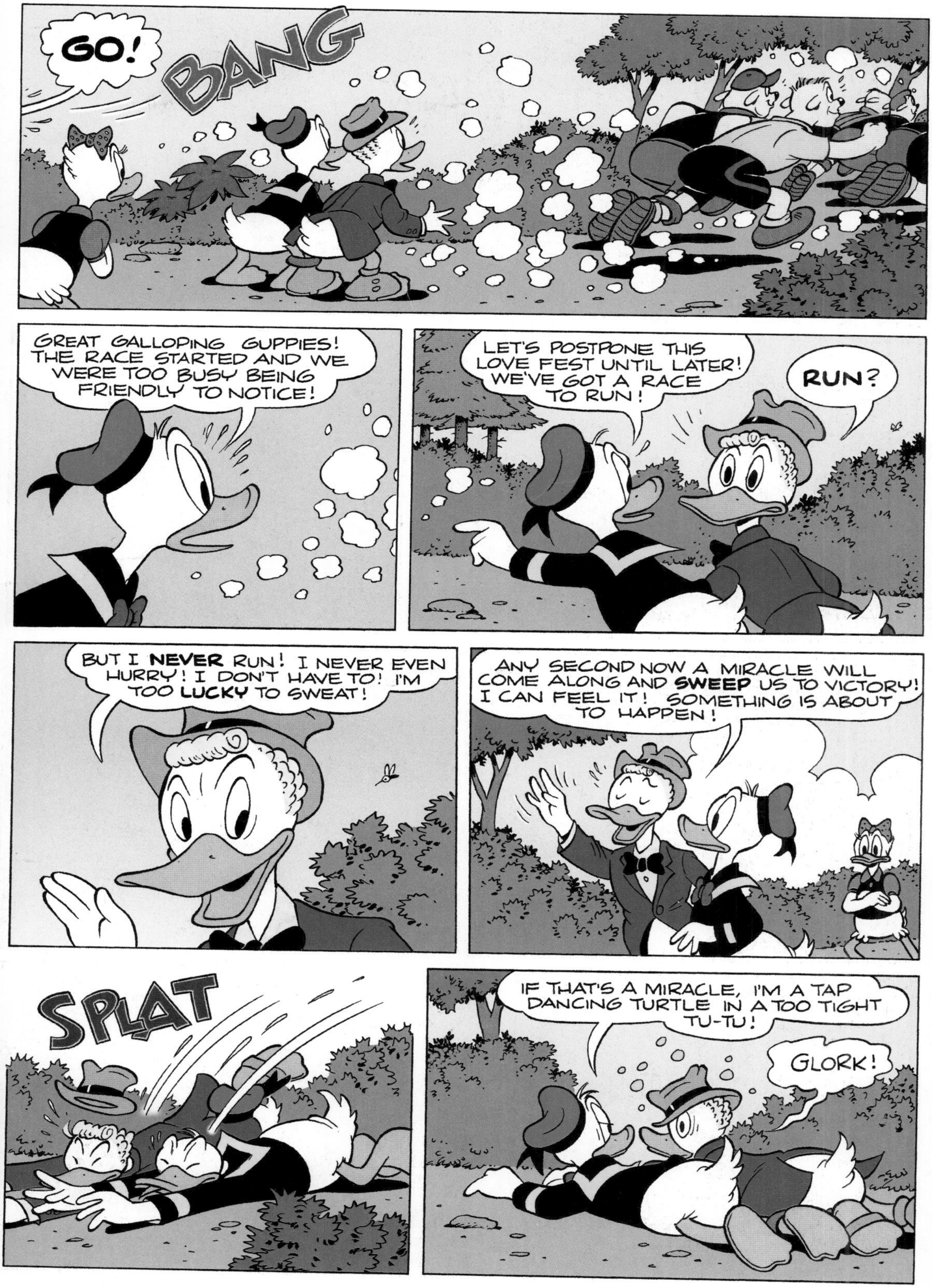

GO!
BANG
GREAT GALLOPING GUPPIES! THE RACE STARTED AND WE WERE TOO BUSY BEING FRIENDLY TO NOTICE!
LET'S POSTPONE THIS LOVE FEST UNTIL LATER! WE'VE GOT A RACE TO RUN!
RUN?
BUT I NEVER RUN! I NEVER EVEN HURRY! I DON'T HAVE TO! I'M TOO LUCKY TO SWEAT!
ANY SECOND NOW A MIRACLE WILL COME ALONG AND SWEEP US TO VICTORY! I CAN FEEL IT! SOMETHING IS ABOUT TO HAPPEN!
SPLAT
IF THAT'S A MIRACLE, I'M A TAP DANCING TURTLE IN A TOO TIGHT TU-TU!
GLORK!

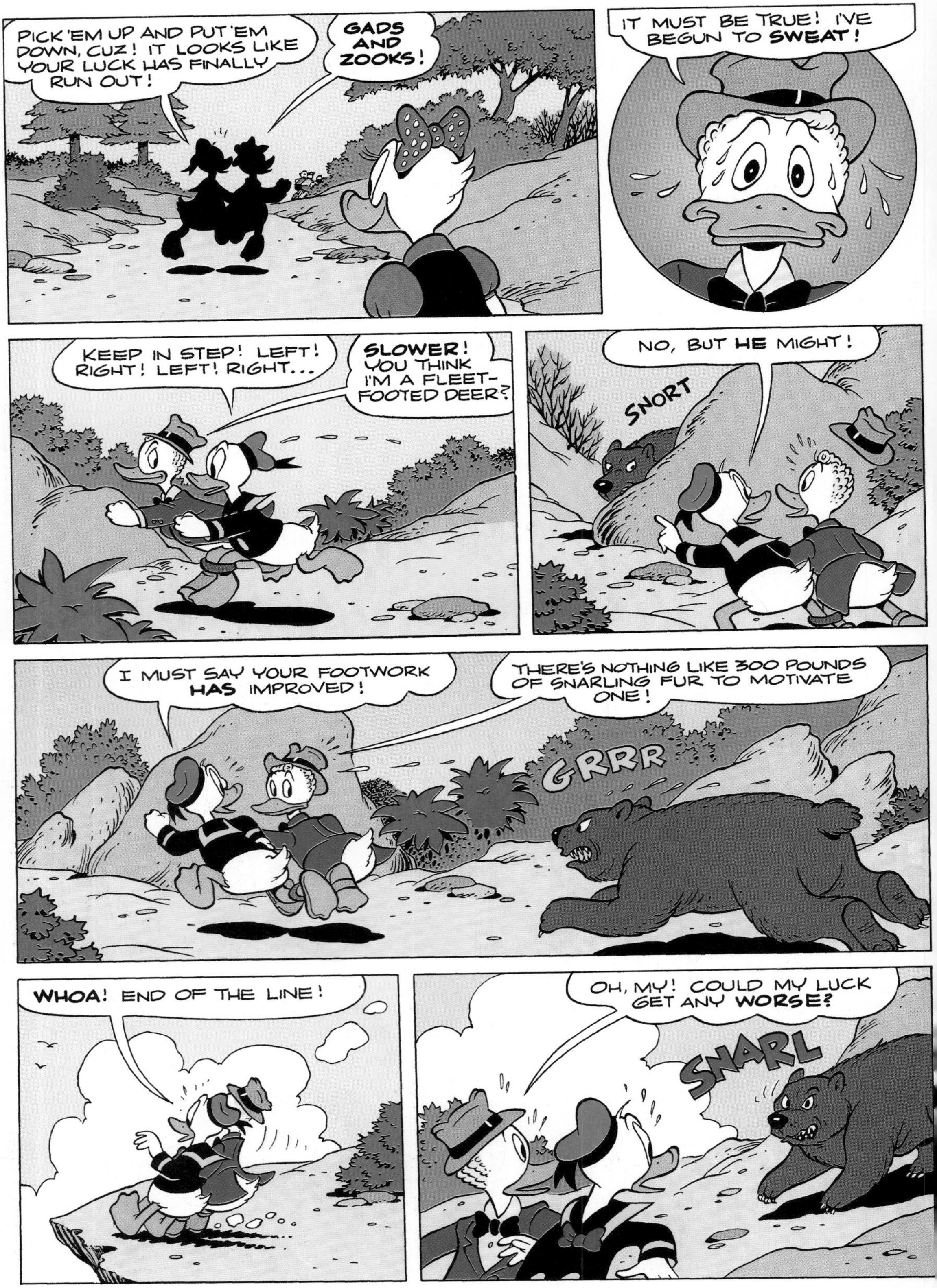

PICK 'EM UP AND PUT 'EM DOWN, CUZ! IT LOOKS LIKE YOUR LUCK HAS FINALLY RUN OUT!
GADS AND ZOOKS!
IT MUST BE TRUE! I'VE BEGUN TO SWEAT!
KEEP IN STEP! LEFT! RIGHT! LEFT! RIGHT...
SLOWER! YOU THINK I'M A FLEET-FOOTED DEER?
NO, BUT HE MIGHT!
SNORT
I MUST SAY YOUR FOOTWORK HAS IMPROVED!
THERE'S NOTHING LIKE 300 POUNDS OF SNARLING FUR TO MOTIVATE ONE!
GRRR
WHOA! END OF THE LINE!
OH, MY! COULD MY LUCK GET ANY WORSE?
SNARL

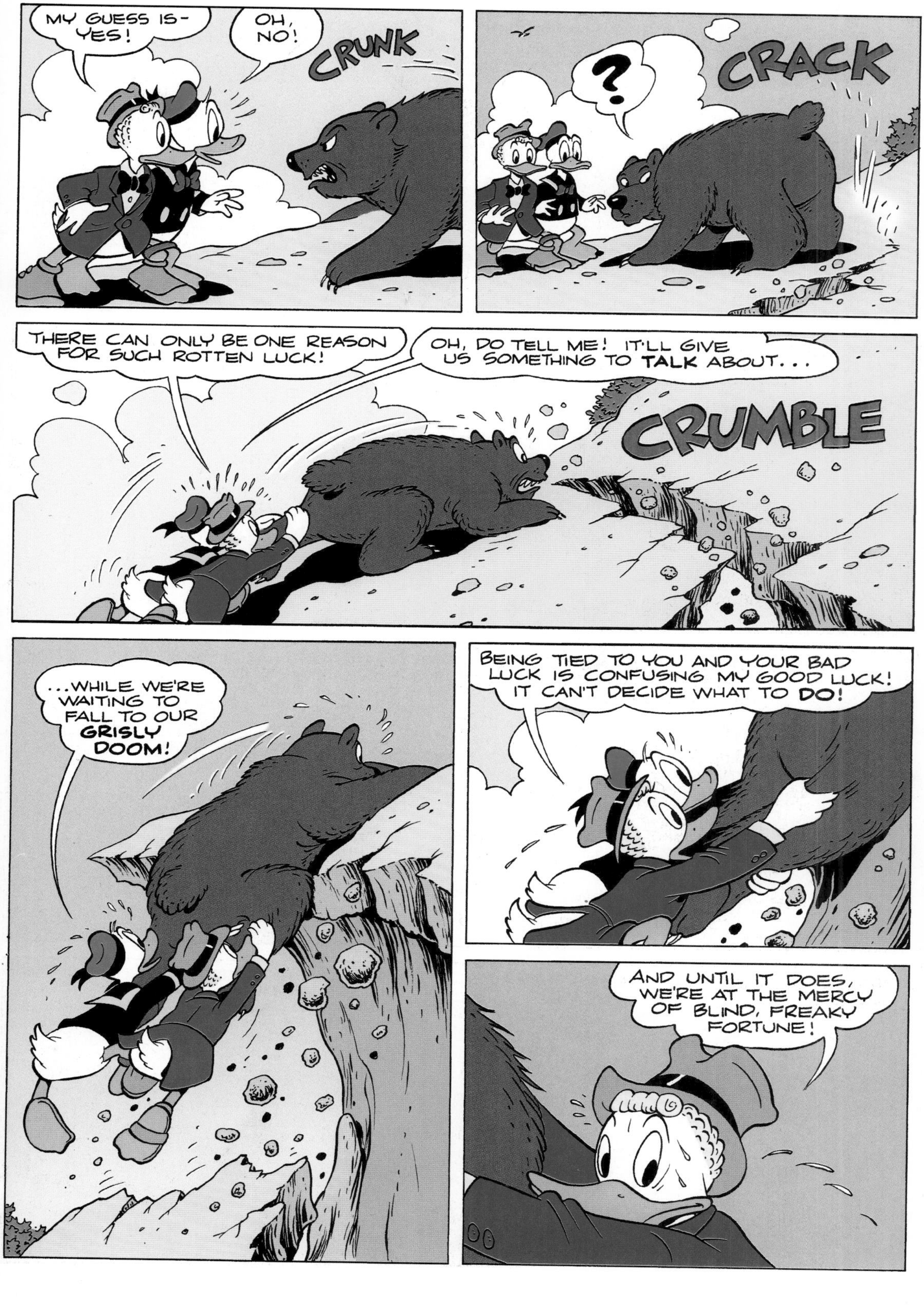

MY GUESS IS- YES!
OH, NO!
CRUNK
?
CRACK
THERE CAN ONLY BE ONE REASON FOR SUCH ROTTEN LUCK!
OH, DO TELL ME! IT'LL GIVE US SOMETHING TO TALK ABOUT...
CRUMBLE
...WHILE WE'RE WAITING TO FALL TO OUR GRISLY DOOM!
BEING TIED TO YOU AND YOUR BAD LUCK IS CONFUSING MY GOOD LUCK! IT CAN'T DECIDE WHAT TO DO!
AND UNTIL IT DOES, WE'RE AT THE MERCY OF BLIND, FREAKY FORTUNE!

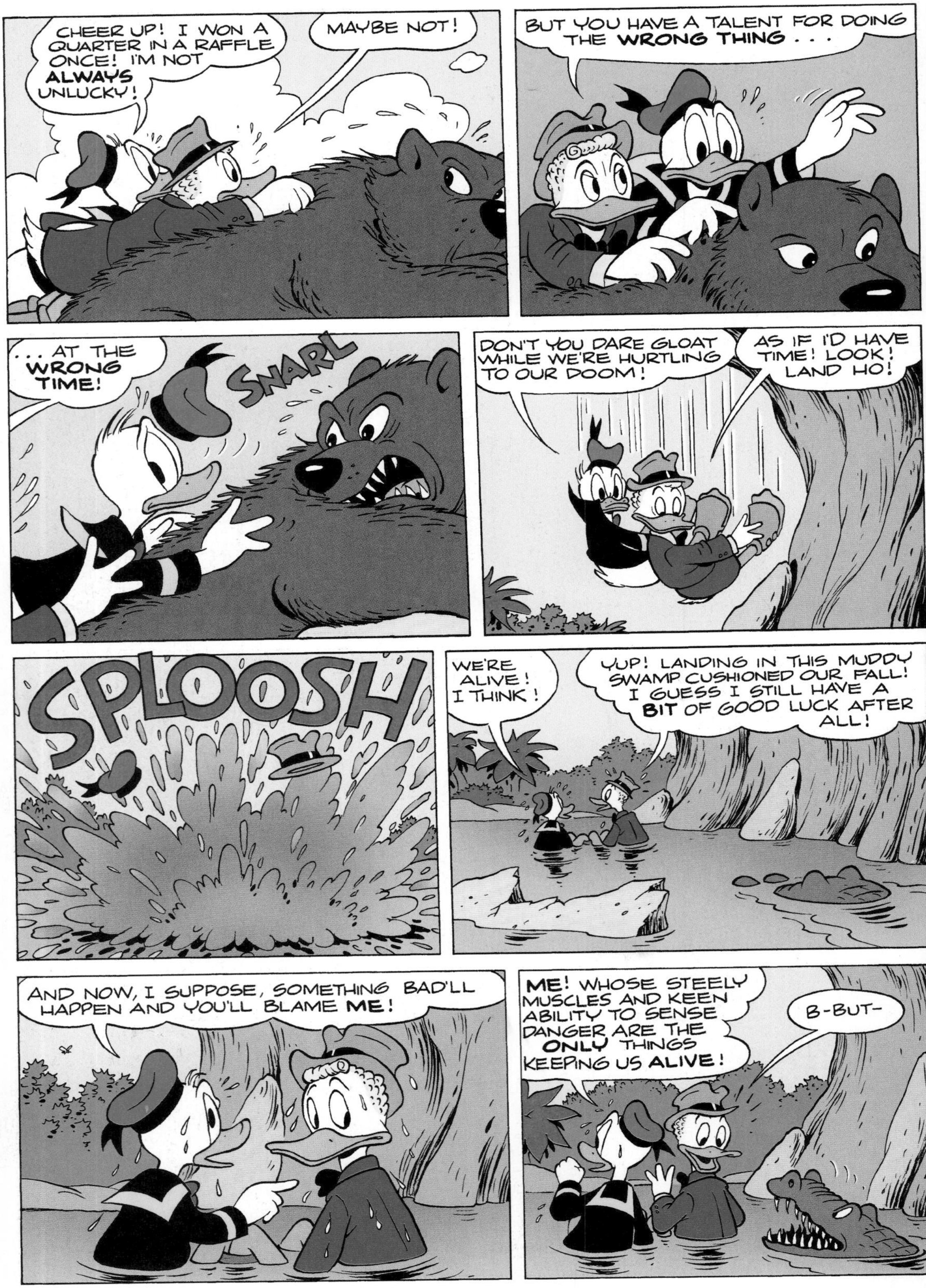
CHEER UP! I WON A QUARTER IN A RAFFLE ONCE! I'M NOT ALWAYS UNLUCKY!
MAYBE NOT!
BUT YOU HAVE A TALENT FOR DOING THE WRONG THING . . .
. . . AT THE WRONG TIME!
SNARL
DON'T YOU DARE GLOAT WHILE WE'RE HURTLING TO OUR DOOM!
AS IF I'D HAVE TIME! LOOK! LAND HO!
SPLOOSH
WE'RE ALIVE! I THINK!
YUP! LANDING IN THIS MUDDY SWAMP CUSHIONED OUR FALL! I GUESS I STILL HAVE A BIT OF GOOD LUCK AFTER ALL!
AND NOW, I SUPPOSE, SOMETHING BAD'LL HAPPEN AND YOU'LL BLAME ME!
ME! WHOSE STEELY MUSCLES AND KEEN ABILITY TO SENSE DANGER ARE THE ONLY THINGS KEEPING US ALIVE!
B-BUT-

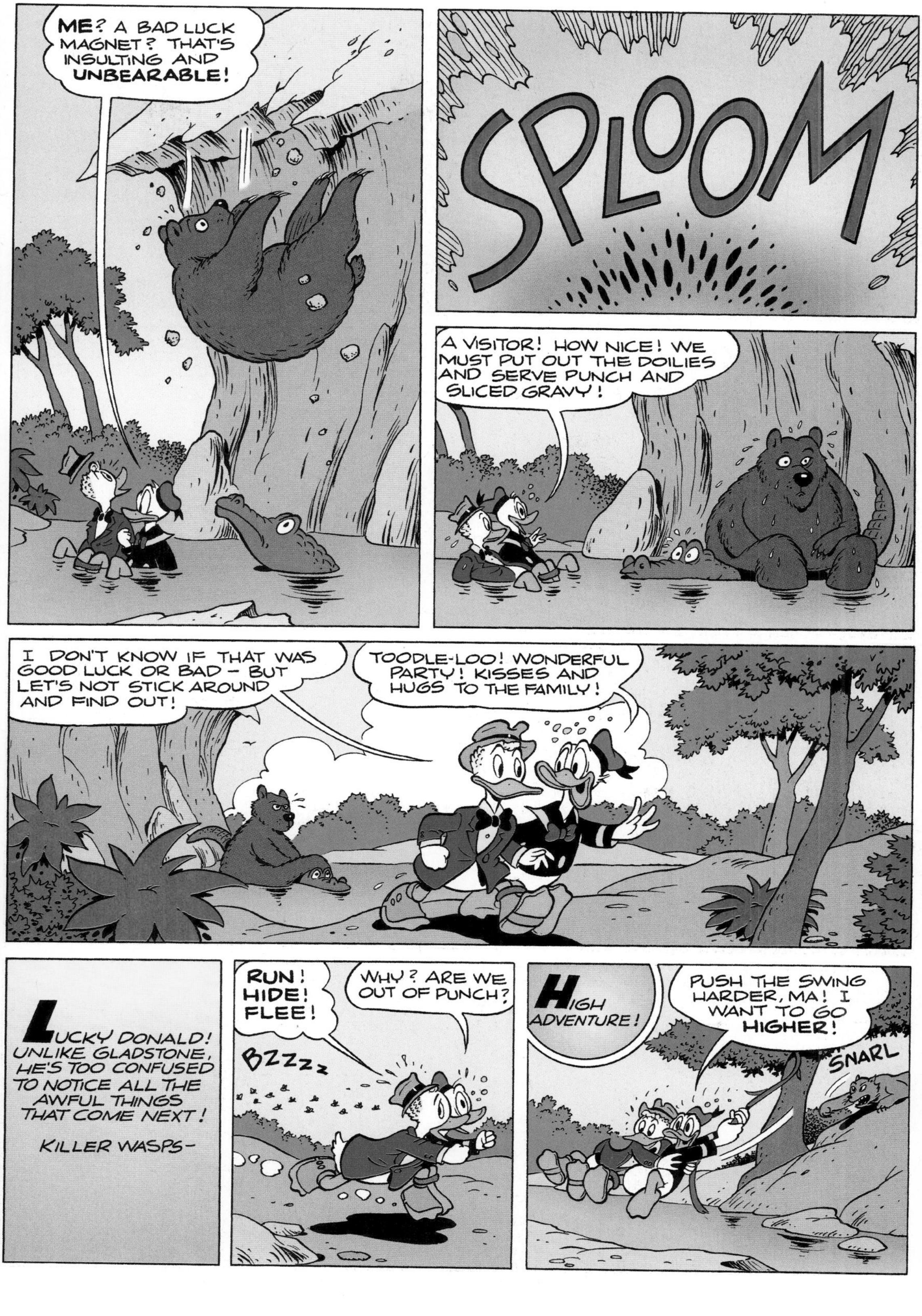

ME? A BAD LUCK MAGNET? THAT'S INSULTING AND UNBEARABLE!
SPLOOM
A VISITOR! HOW NICE! WE MUST PUT OUT THE DOILIES AND SERVE PUNCH AND SLICED GRAVY!
I DON'T KNOW IF THAT WAS GOOD LUCK OR BAD – BUT LET'S NOT STICK AROUND AND FIND OUT!
TOODLE-LOO! WONDERFUL PARTY! KISSES AND HUGS TO THE FAMILY!
LUCKY DONALD! UNLIKE GLADSTONE, HE'S TOO CONFUSED TO NOTICE ALL THE AWFUL THINGS THAT COME NEXT!
KILLER WASPS–
RUN! HIDE! FLEE!
WHY? ARE WE OUT OF PUNCH?
BZZzzz
HIGH ADVENTURE!
PUSH THE SWING HARDER, MA! I WANT TO GO HIGHER!
SNARL

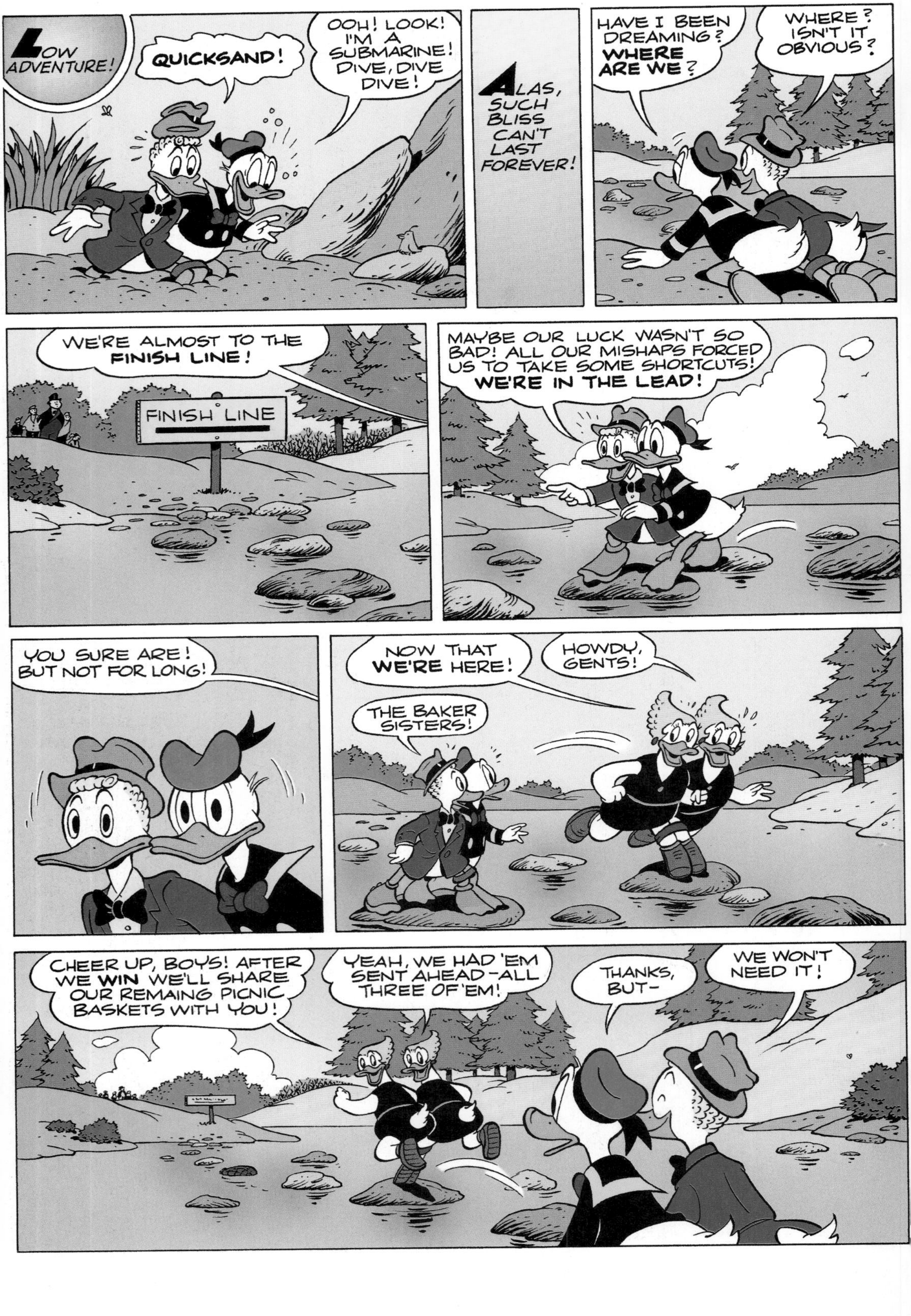
LOW ADVENTURE!
QUICKSAND!
OOH! LOOK! I'M A SUBMARINE! DIVE, DIVE DIVE!
ALAS, SUCH BLISS CAN'T LAST FOREVER!
HAVE I BEEN DREAMING? WHERE ARE WE?
WHERE? ISN'T IT OBVIOUS?
WE'RE ALMOST TO THE FINISH LINE!
FINISH LINE
MAYBE OUR LUCK WASN'T SO BAD! ALL OUR MISHAPS FORCED US TO TAKE SOME SHORTCUTS! WE'RE IN THE LEAD!
YOU SURE ARE! BUT NOT FOR LONG!
NOW THAT WE'RE HERE!
HOWDY, GENTS!
THE BAKER SISTERS!
CHEER UP, BOYS! AFTER WE WIN WE'LL SHARE OUR REMAING PICNIC BASKETS WITH YOU!
YEAH, WE HAD 'EM SENT AHEAD-ALL THREE OF 'EM!
THANKS, BUT-
WE WON'T NEED IT!

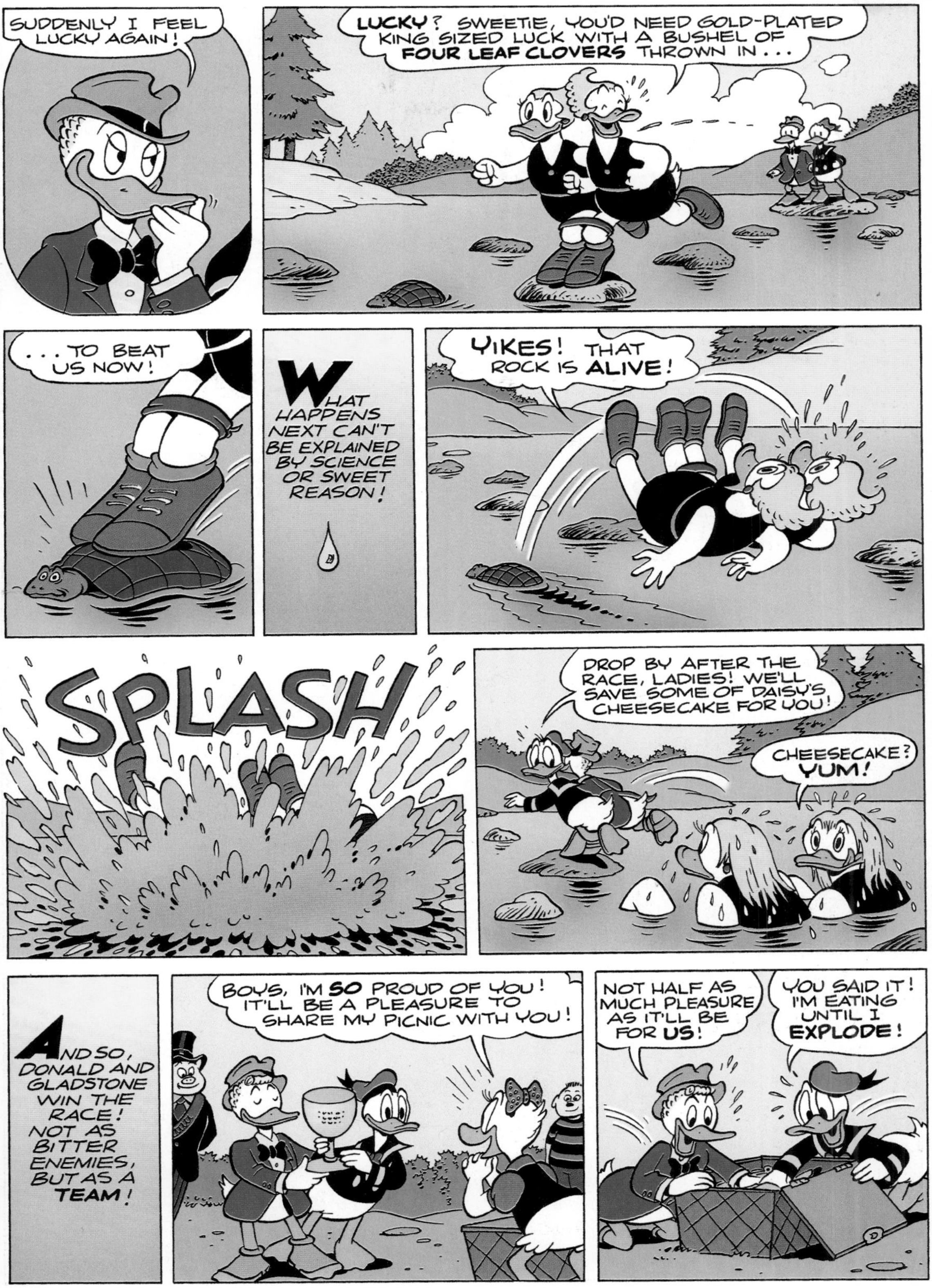
SUDDENLY I FEEL LUCKY AGAIN!
LUCKY? SWEETIE, YOU'D NEED GOLD-PLATED KING SIZED LUCK WITH A BUSHEL OF FOUR LEAF CLOVERS THROWN IN . . .
. . . TO BEAT US NOW!
WHAT HAPPENS NEXT CAN'T BE EXPLAINED BY SCIENCE OR SWEET REASON!
YIKES! THAT ROCK IS ALIVE!
SPLASH
DROP BY AFTER THE RACE, LADIES! WE'LL SAVE SOME OF DAISY'S CHEESECAKE FOR YOU!
CHEESECAKE? YUM!
AND SO, DONALD AND GLADSTONE WIN THE RACE! NOT AS BITTER ENEMIES, BUT AS A TEAM!
BOYS, I'M SO PROUD OF YOU! IT'LL BE A PLEASURE TO SHARE MY PICNIC WITH YOU!
NOT HALF AS MUCH PLEASURE AS IT'LL BE FOR US!
YOU SAID IT! I'M EATING UNTIL I EXPLODE!

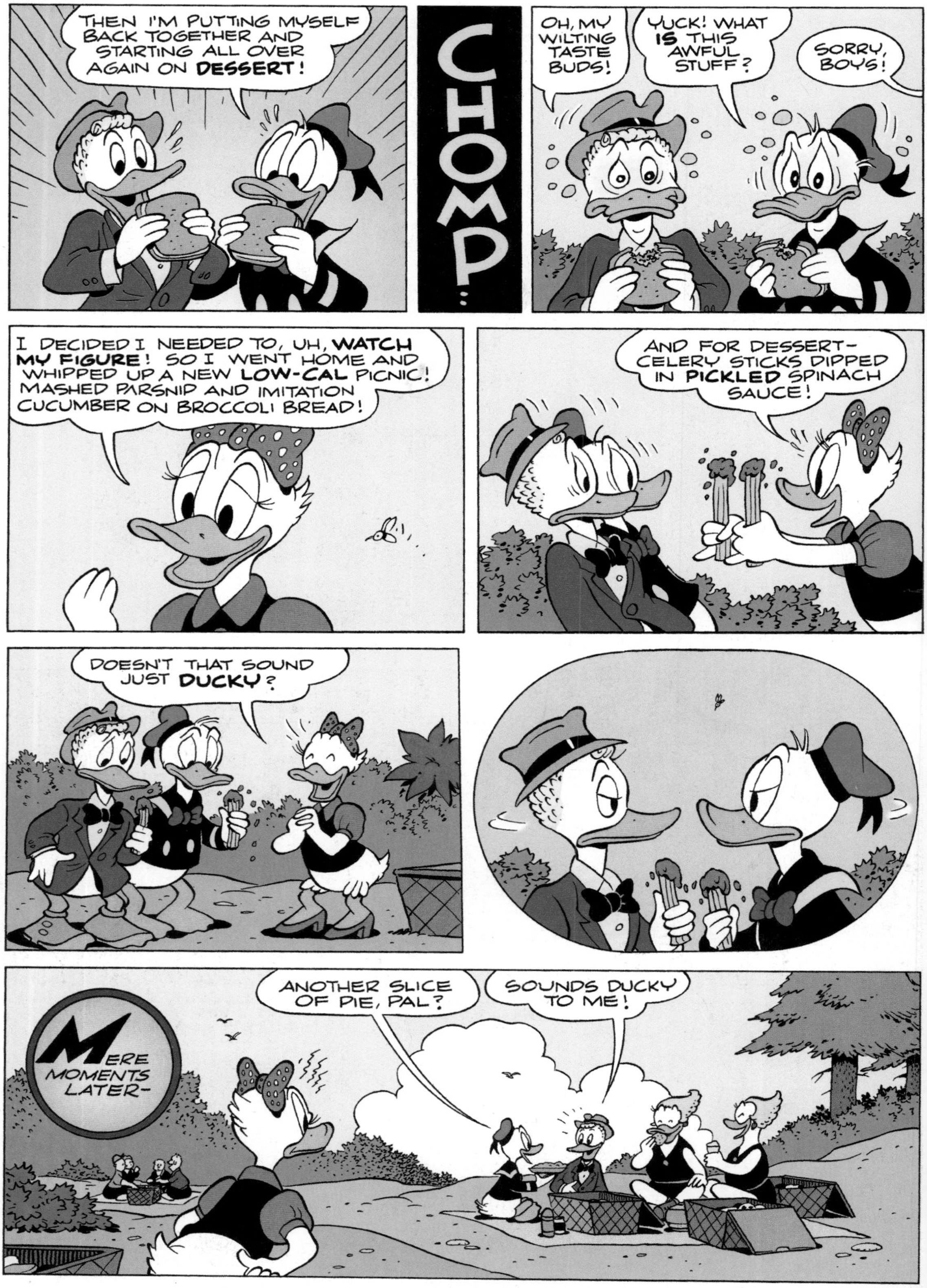

THEN I'M PUTTING MYSELF BACK TOGETHER AND STARTING ALL OVER AGAIN ON **DESSERT**!
CHOMP!
OH, MY WILTING TASTE BUDS!
YUCK! WHAT **IS** THIS AWFUL STUFF?
SORRY, BOYS!
I DECIDED I NEEDED TO, UH, **WATCH MY FIGURE**! SO I WENT HOME AND WHIPPED UP A NEW **LOW-CAL** PICNIC! MASHED PARSNIP AND IMITATION CUCUMBER ON BROCCOLI BREAD!
AND FOR DESSERT-CELERY STICKS DIPPED IN **PICKLED** SPINACH SAUCE!
DOESN'T THAT SOUND JUST **DUCKY**?
MERE MOMENTS LATER-
ANOTHER SLICE OF PIE, PAL?
SOUNDS DUCKY TO ME!

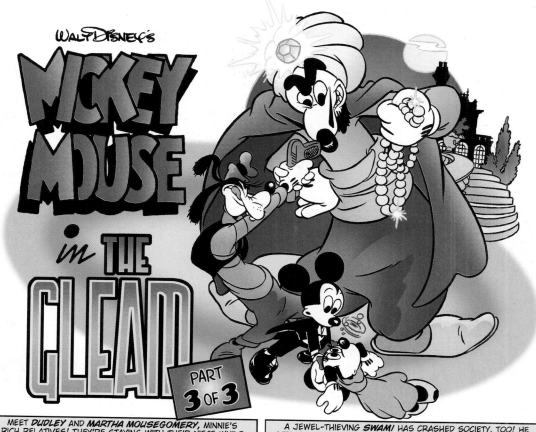

Walt Disney's

MICKEY MOUSE

in THE GLEAM

MEET *DUDLEY* AND *MARTHA MOUSEGOMERY*, MINNIE'S RICH RELATIVES! THEY'RE STAYING WITH THEIR NIECE WHILE THEY CRASH MOUSETON SOCIETY!

I'M SO THRILLED TO BE GOING TO THE VAN SWANK'S PARTY!

ENTERTAINING PEOPLE, MINNIE?

AREN'T WE LUCKY THAT YOU KNOW SUCH

YEP... CAN'T HAVE TOO MANY PARTIES TO SUIT ME, DADGUMMIT!

YM 048

A JEWEL-THIEVING *SWAMI* HAS CRASHED SOCIETY, TOO! HE STRIKES AT EVERY PARTY MINNIE'S RELATIVES ATTEND... HELPED BY A MYSTERIOUS *PARTNER* WHOM NO ONE EVER *SEES!*

RIGHT IN MY OWN DRAWING-ROOM! OHH-H!

DREADFUL!

THERE OUGHT TO BE A LAW!

THE COPS ARE OUTSIDE! I'LL GO SEE IF ...!

WHEN MICKEY AND DETECTIVE CASEY INVESTIGATE, MICKEY LEARNS THAT *SOMEHOW,* THE "GLEAM'S" PARTNER IS... *MINNIE!*

WHAT? HOW? WHY?

CHIEF O'HARA SPEAKIN' DID YE PROVE WHAT YE WANTED TO AT THE PARTY LAST NIGHT?

Y-YES...I MEAN, **NO!** I MEAN, UH ...NOTHIN' EXACTLY **DEFINITE**!

MINNIE INSISTS SHE'S NOT INVOLVED IN THE ROBBERIES... AND MICKEY IS CONVINCED SHE'S NOT KNOWINGLY LYING! BUT BEFORE MICKEY CAN SORT *MINNIE'S* MIND OUT — HIS *OWN* BRAIN GOES FOR A WALK ON THE FLIP SIDE...

OOP! OOP! I'M A CHIMPANZEE!

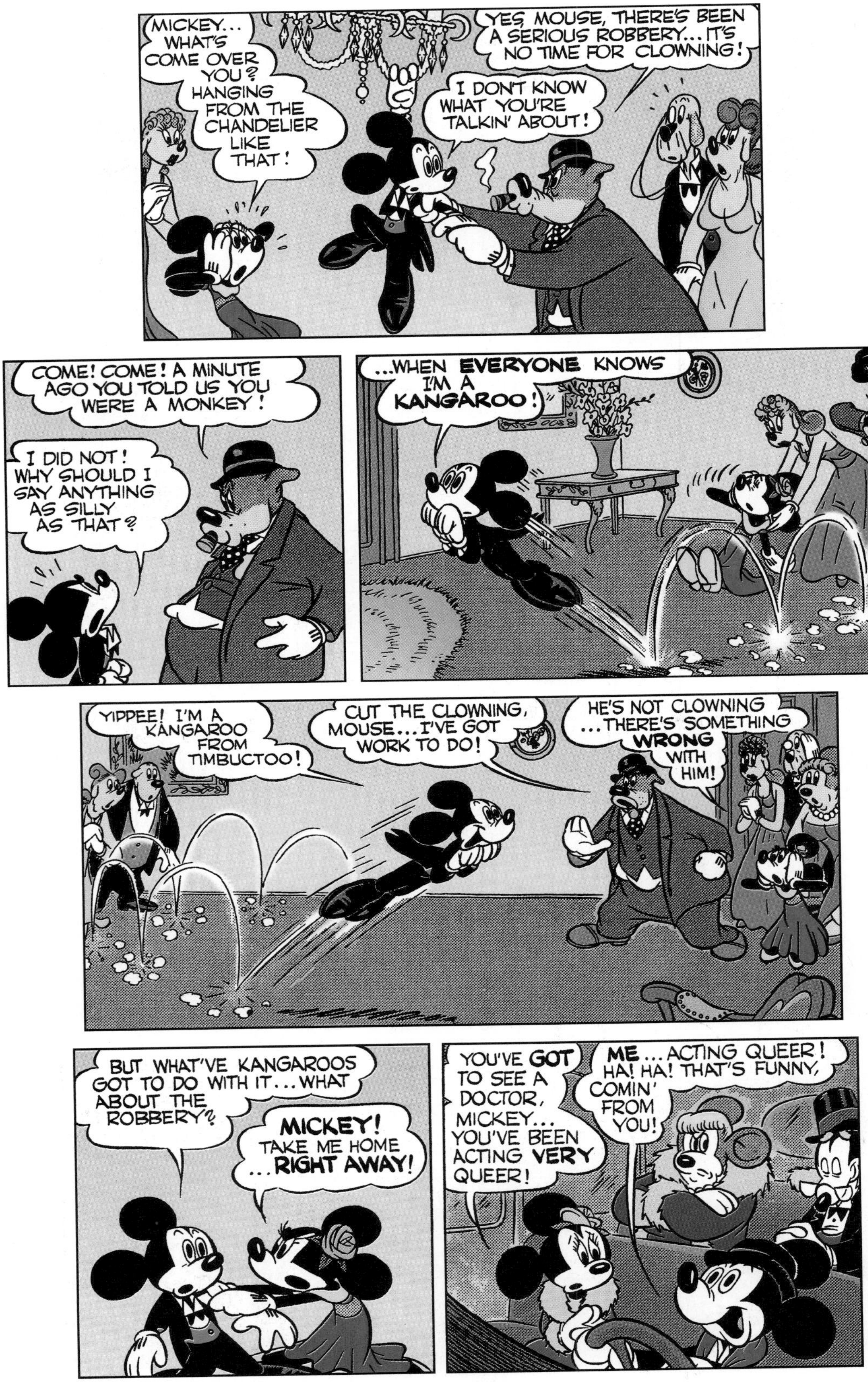
MICKEY... WHAT'S COME OVER YOU? HANGING FROM THE CHANDELIER LIKE THAT!
I DON'T KNOW WHAT YOU'RE TALKIN' ABOUT!
YES MOUSE, THERE'S BEEN A SERIOUS ROBBERY... IT'S NO TIME FOR CLOWNING!
COME! COME! A MINUTE AGO YOU TOLD US YOU WERE A MONKEY!
I DID NOT! WHY SHOULD I SAY ANYTHING AS SILLY AS THAT?
...WHEN EVERYONE KNOWS I'M A KANGAROO!
YIPPEE! I'M A KANGAROO FROM TIMBUCTOO!
CUT THE CLOWNING, MOUSE... I'VE GOT WORK TO DO!
HE'S NOT CLOWNING ...THERE'S SOMETHING WRONG WITH HIM!
BUT WHAT'VE KANGAROOS GOT TO DO WITH IT... WHAT ABOUT THE ROBBERY?
MICKEY! TAKE ME HOME ...RIGHT AWAY!
YOU'VE GOT TO SEE A DOCTOR, MICKEY... YOU'VE BEEN ACTING VERY QUEER!
ME... ACTING QUEER! HA! HA! THAT'S FUNNY, COMIN' FROM YOU!

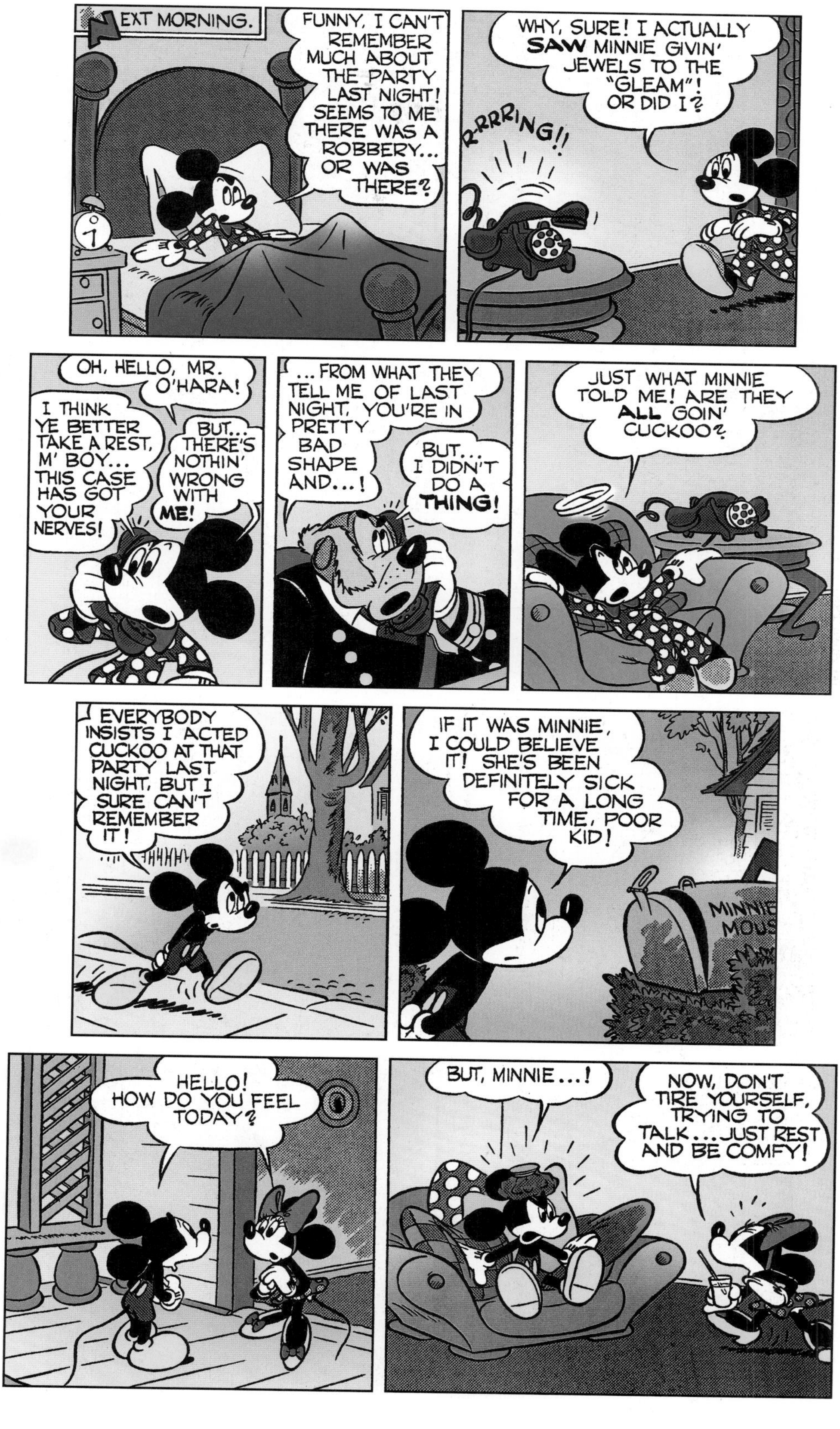
NEXT MORNING.
FUNNY, I CAN'T REMEMBER MUCH ABOUT THE PARTY LAST NIGHT! SEEMS TO ME THERE WAS A ROBBERY... OR WAS THERE?
WHY, SURE! I ACTUALLY SAW MINNIE GIVIN' JEWELS TO THE "GLEAM"! OR DID I?
R-RRRING!!
OH, HELLO, MR. O'HARA!
I THINK YE BETTER TAKE A REST, M' BOY... THIS CASE HAS GOT YOUR NERVES!
BUT... THERE'S NOTHIN' WRONG WITH ME!
... FROM WHAT THEY TELL ME OF LAST NIGHT, YOU'RE IN PRETTY BAD SHAPE AND...!
BUT... I DIDN'T DO A THING!
JUST WHAT MINNIE TOLD ME! ARE THEY ALL GOIN' CUCKOO?
EVERYBODY INSISTS I ACTED CUCKOO AT THAT PARTY LAST NIGHT, BUT I SURE CAN'T REMEMBER IT!
IF IT WAS MINNIE, I COULD BELIEVE IT! SHE'S BEEN DEFINITELY SICK FOR A LONG TIME, POOR KID!
MINNIE MOUS
HELLO! HOW DO YOU FEEL TODAY?
BUT, MINNIE...!
NOW, DON'T TIRE YOURSELF, TRYING TO TALK... JUST REST AND BE COMFY!

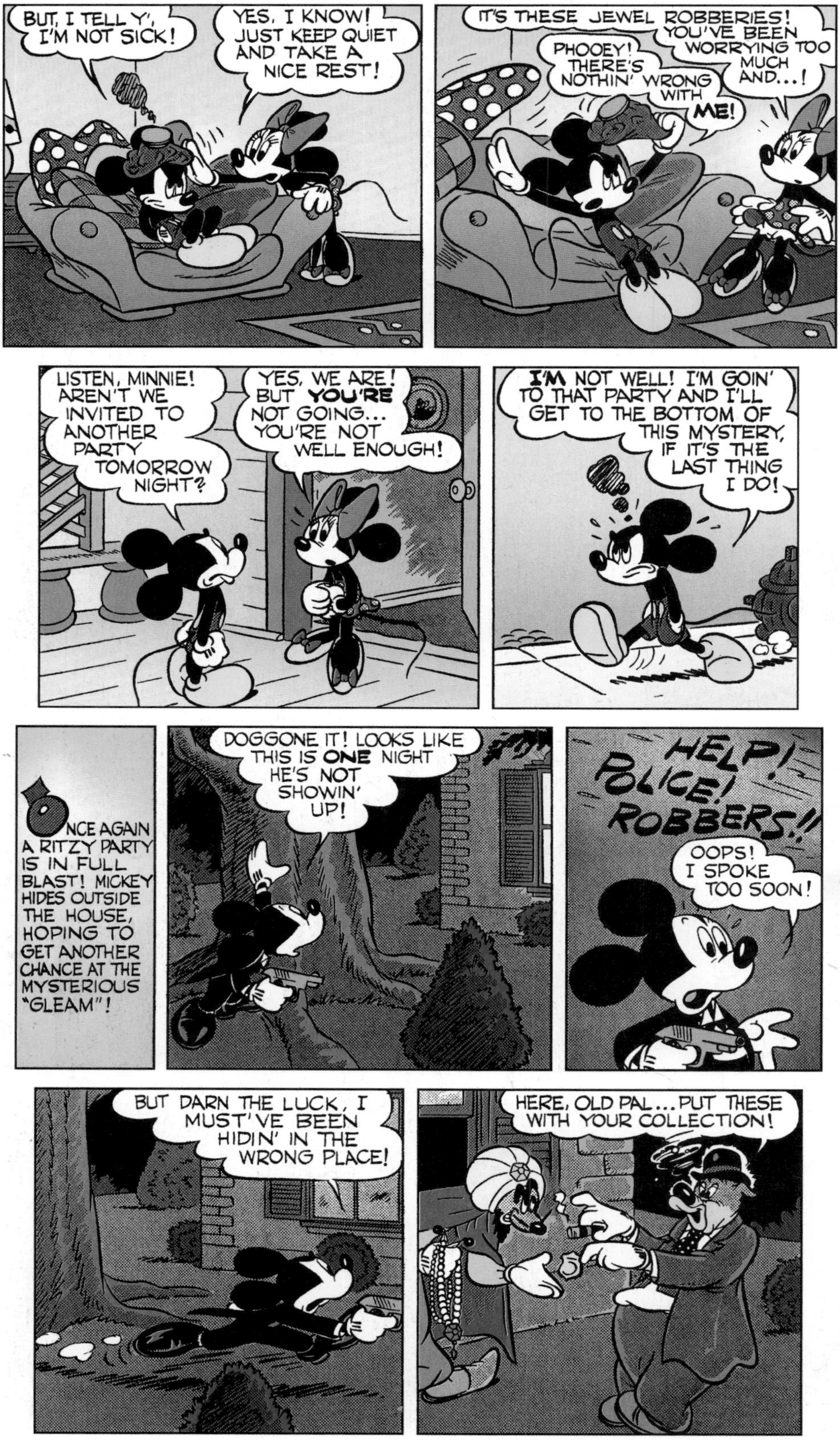
BUT, I TELL Y', I'M NOT SICK!
YES, I KNOW! JUST KEEP QUIET AND TAKE A NICE REST!
IT'S THESE JEWEL ROBBERIES! YOU'VE BEEN WORRYING TOO MUCH AND...!
PHOOEY! THERE'S NOTHIN' WRONG WITH ME!
LISTEN, MINNIE! AREN'T WE INVITED TO ANOTHER PARTY TOMORROW NIGHT?
YES, WE ARE! BUT YOU'RE NOT GOING... YOU'RE NOT WELL ENOUGH!
I'M NOT WELL! I'M GOIN' TO THAT PARTY AND I'LL GET TO THE BOTTOM OF THIS MYSTERY, IF IT'S THE LAST THING I DO!
ONCE AGAIN A RITZY PARTY IS IN FULL BLAST! MICKEY HIDES OUTSIDE THE HOUSE, HOPING TO GET ANOTHER CHANCE AT THE MYSTERIOUS "GLEAM"!
DOGGONE IT! LOOKS LIKE THIS IS ONE NIGHT HE'S NOT SHOWIN' UP!
HELP! POLICE! ROBBERS!!
OOPS! I SPOKE TOO SOON!
BUT DARN THE LUCK, I MUST'VE BEEN HIDIN' IN THE WRONG PLACE!
HERE, OLD PAL... PUT THESE WITH YOUR COLLECTION!

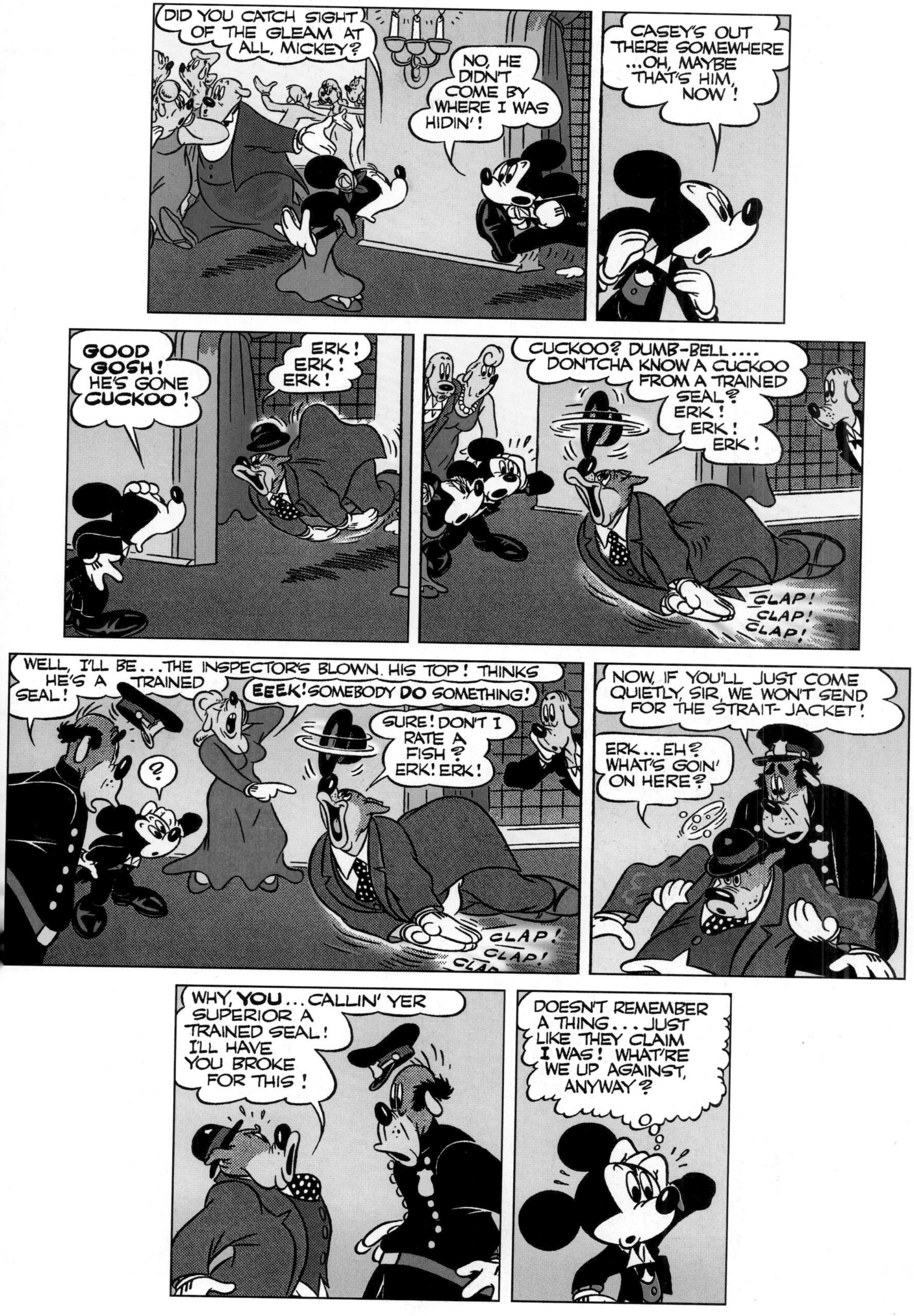
DID YOU CATCH SIGHT OF THE GLEAM AT ALL, MICKEY?
NO, HE DIDN'T COME BY WHERE I WAS HIDIN'!
CASEY'S OUT THERE SOMEWHERE ...OH, MAYBE THAT'S HIM, NOW!
GOOD GOSH! HE'S GONE CUCKOO!
ERK! ERK! ERK!
CUCKOO? DUMB-BELL.... DON'TCHA KNOW A CUCKOO FROM A TRAINED SEAL? ERK! ERK! ERK!
CLAP! CLAP! CLAP!
WELL, I'LL BE...THE INSPECTOR'S BLOWN HIS TOP! THINKS HE'S A TRAINED SEAL!
EEEK! SOMEBODY DO SOMETHING!
?
SURE! DON'T I RATE A FISH? ERK! ERK!
CLAP! CLAP!
NOW, IF YOU'LL JUST COME QUIETLY, SIR, WE WON'T SEND FOR THE STRAIT-JACKET!
ERK...EH? WHAT'S GOIN' ON HERE?
WHY, YOU...CALLIN' YER SUPERIOR A TRAINED SEAL! I'LL HAVE YOU BROKE FOR THIS!
DOESN'T REMEMBER A THING... JUST LIKE THEY CLAIM I WAS! WHAT'RE WE UP AGAINST, ANYWAY?

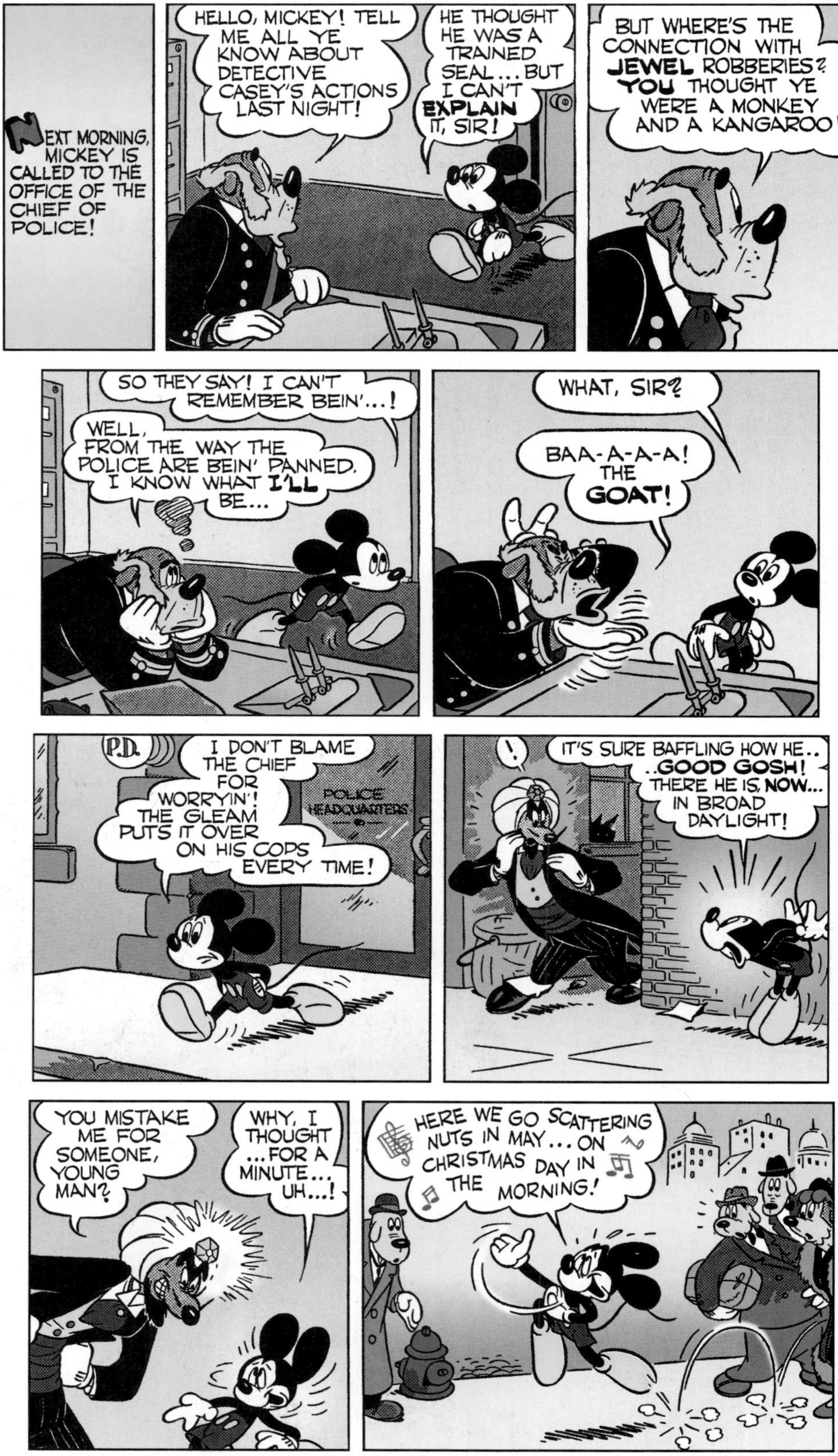
NEXT MORNING, MICKEY IS CALLED TO THE OFFICE OF THE CHIEF OF POLICE!
HELLO, MICKEY! TELL ME ALL YE KNOW ABOUT DETECTIVE CASEY'S ACTIONS LAST NIGHT!
HE THOUGHT HE WAS A TRAINED SEAL... BUT I CAN'T EXPLAIN IT, SIR!
BUT WHERE'S THE CONNECTION WITH JEWEL ROBBERIES? YOU THOUGHT YE WERE A MONKEY AND A KANGAROO!
SO THEY SAY! I CAN'T REMEMBER BEIN'...!
WELL, FROM THE WAY THE POLICE ARE BEIN' PANNED, I KNOW WHAT I'LL BE...
WHAT, SIR?
BAA-A-A-A! THE GOAT!
P.D.
I DON'T BLAME THE CHIEF FOR WORRYIN'! THE GLEAM PUTS IT OVER ON HIS COPS EVERY TIME!
POLICE HEADQUARTERS
!
IT'S SURE BAFFLING HOW HE.. ..GOOD GOSH! THERE HE IS, NOW... IN BROAD DAYLIGHT!
YOU MISTAKE ME FOR SOMEONE, YOUNG MAN?
WHY, I THOUGHT ...FOR A MINUTE... UH...!
HERE WE GO SCATTERING NUTS IN MAY... ON CHRISTMAS DAY IN THE MORNING!

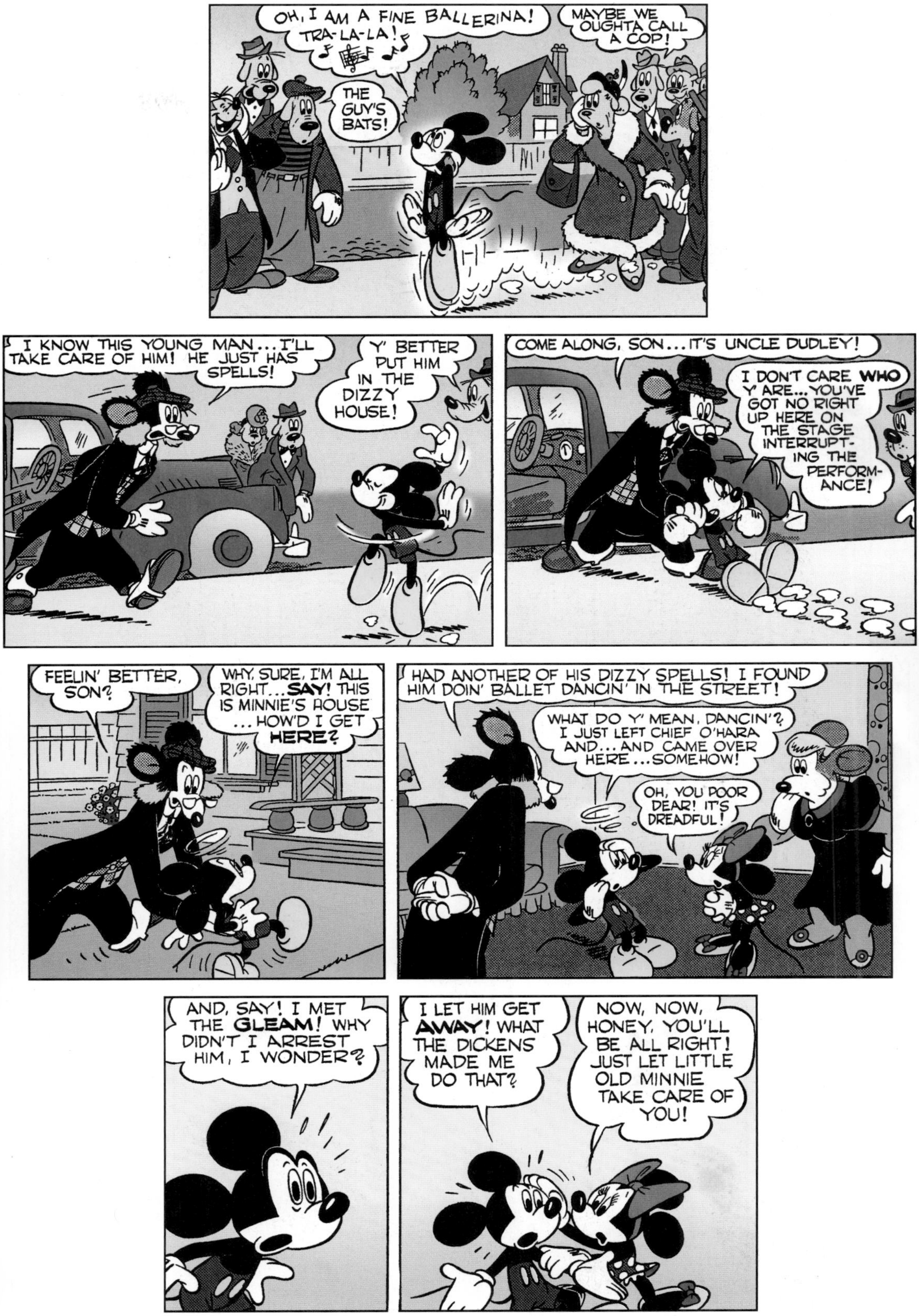
OH, I AM A FINE BALLERINA! TRA-LA-LA!
THE GUY'S BATS!
MAYBE WE OUGHTA CALL A COP!
I KNOW THIS YOUNG MAN... I'LL TAKE CARE OF HIM! HE JUST HAS SPELLS!
Y' BETTER PUT HIM IN THE DIZZY HOUSE!
COME ALONG, SON... IT'S UNCLE DUDLEY!
I DON'T CARE WHO Y' ARE... YOU'VE GOT NO RIGHT UP HERE ON THE STAGE INTERRUPTING THE PERFORMANCE!
FEELIN' BETTER, SON?
WHY, SURE, I'M ALL RIGHT... SAY! THIS IS MINNIE'S HOUSE ... HOW'D I GET HERE?
HAD ANOTHER OF HIS DIZZY SPELLS! I FOUND HIM DOIN' BALLET DANCIN' IN THE STREET!
WHAT DO Y' MEAN, DANCIN'? I JUST LEFT CHIEF O'HARA AND... AND CAME OVER HERE... SOMEHOW!
OH, YOU POOR DEAR! IT'S DREADFUL!
AND, SAY! I MET THE GLEAM! WHY DIDN'T I ARREST HIM, I WONDER?
I LET HIM GET AWAY! WHAT THE DICKENS MADE ME DO THAT?
NOW, NOW, HONEY, YOU'LL BE ALL RIGHT! JUST LET LITTLE OLD MINNIE TAKE CARE OF YOU!

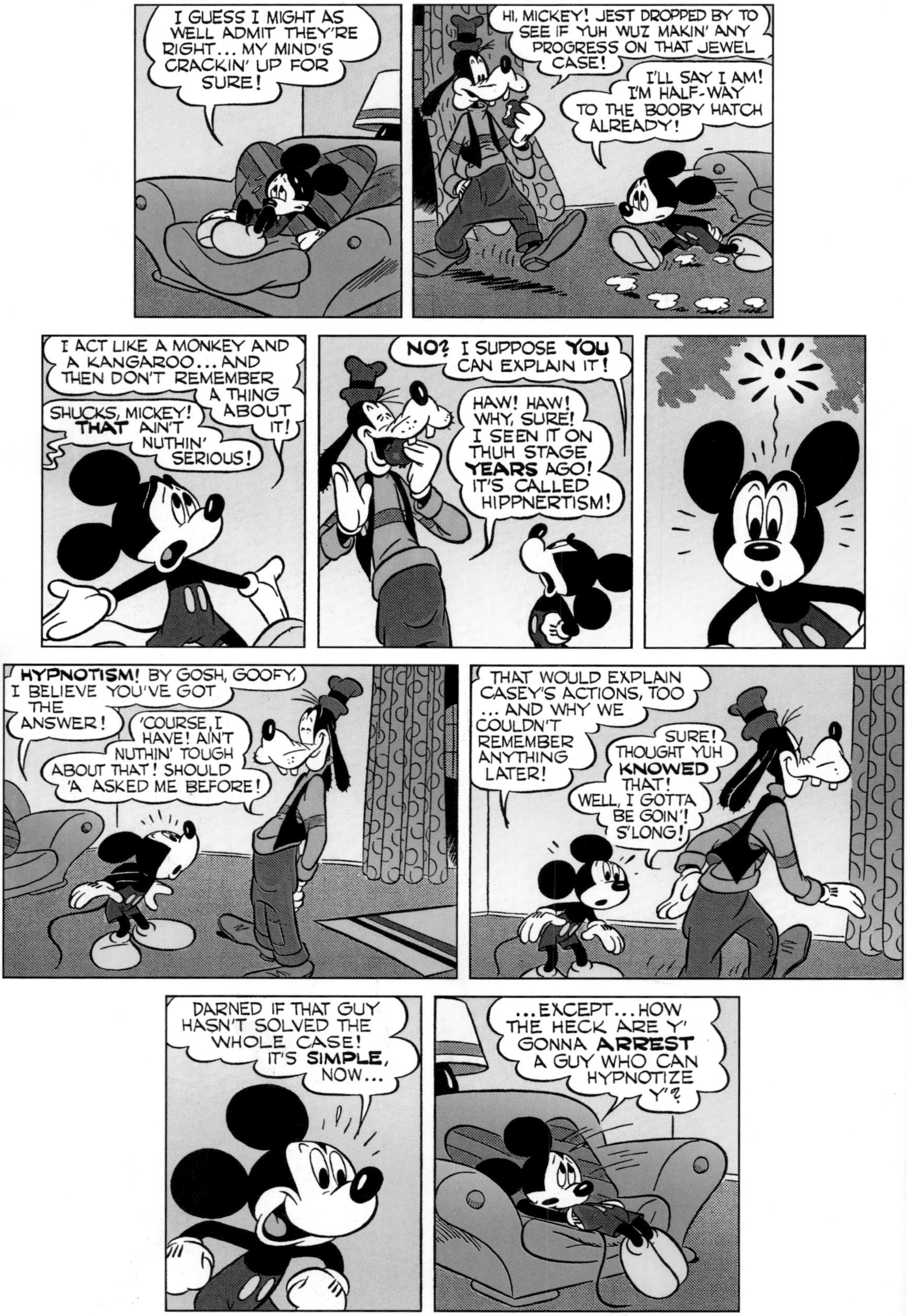
I GUESS I MIGHT AS WELL ADMIT THEY'RE RIGHT... MY MIND'S CRACKIN' UP FOR SURE!
HI, MICKEY! JEST DROPPED BY TO SEE IF YUH WUZ MAKIN' ANY PROGRESS ON THAT JEWEL CASE!
I'LL SAY I AM! I'M HALF-WAY TO THE BOOBY HATCH ALREADY!
I ACT LIKE A MONKEY AND A KANGAROO... AND THEN DON'T REMEMBER A THING ABOUT IT!
SHUCKS, MICKEY! THAT AIN'T NUTHIN' SERIOUS!
NO? I SUPPOSE YOU CAN EXPLAIN IT!
HAW! HAW! WHY, SURE! I SEEN IT ON THUH STAGE YEARS AGO! IT'S CALLED HIPPNERTISM!
HYPNOTISM! BY GOSH, GOOFY, I BELIEVE YOU'VE GOT THE ANSWER!
'COURSE, I HAVE! AIN'T NUTHIN' TOUGH ABOUT THAT! SHOULD 'A ASKED ME BEFORE!
THAT WOULD EXPLAIN CASEY'S ACTIONS, TOO ... AND WHY WE COULDN'T REMEMBER ANYTHING LATER!
SURE! THOUGHT YUH KNOWED THAT! WELL, I GOTTA BE GOIN'! S'LONG!
DARNED IF THAT GUY HASN'T SOLVED THE WHOLE CASE! IT'S SIMPLE, NOW...
...EXCEPT... HOW THE HECK ARE Y' GONNA ARREST A GUY WHO CAN HYPNOTIZE Y'?

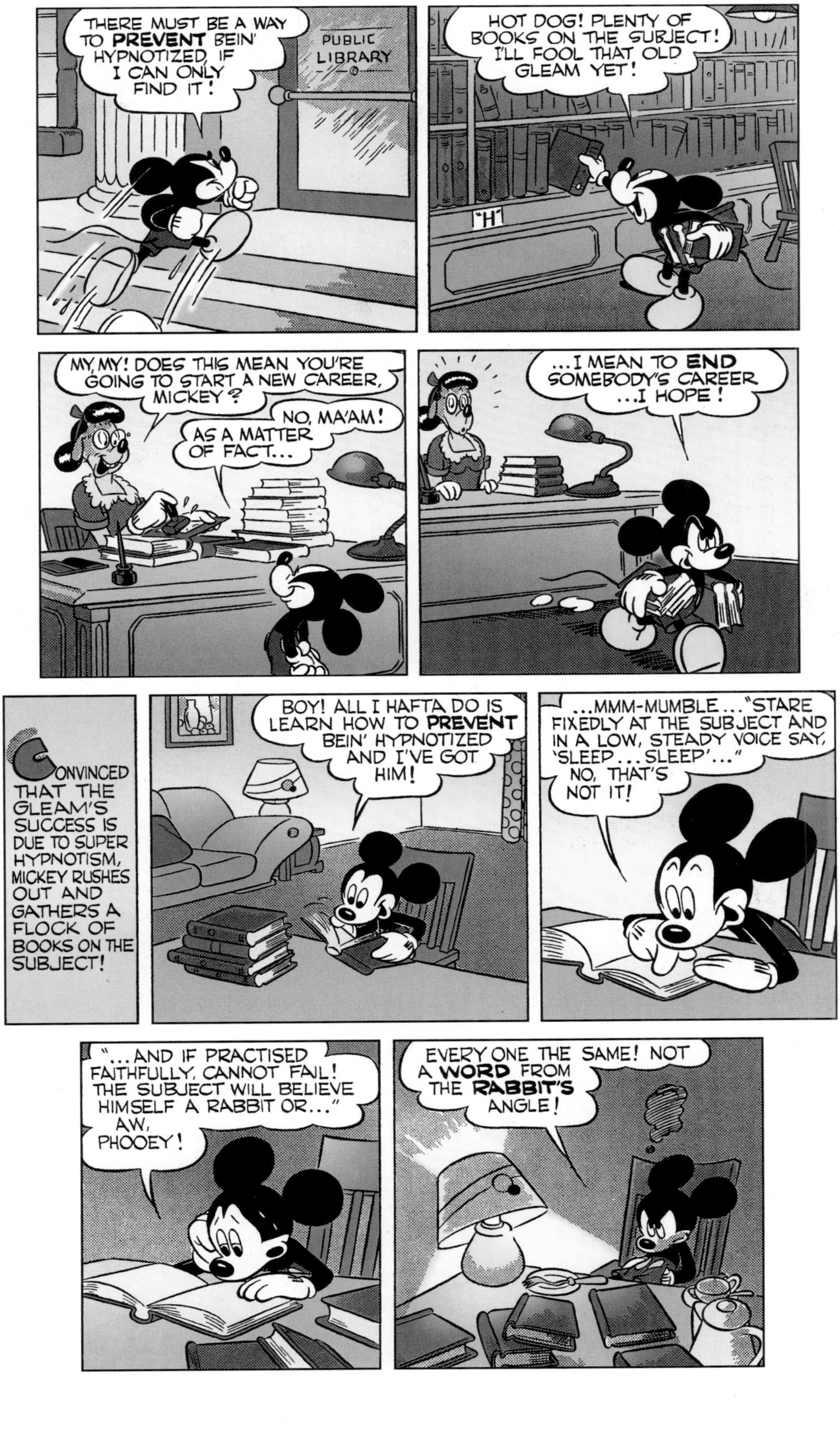
THERE MUST BE A WAY TO PREVENT BEIN' HYPNOTIZED, IF I CAN ONLY FIND IT!
PUBLIC LIBRARY
HOT DOG! PLENTY OF BOOKS ON THE SUBJECT! I'LL FOOL THAT OLD GLEAM YET!
"H"
MY, MY! DOES THIS MEAN YOU'RE GOING TO START A NEW CAREER, MICKEY?
NO, MA'AM! AS A MATTER OF FACT...
...I MEAN TO END SOMEBODY'S CAREER ...I HOPE!
CONVINCED THAT THE GLEAM'S SUCCESS IS DUE TO SUPER HYPNOTISM, MICKEY RUSHES OUT AND GATHERS A FLOCK OF BOOKS ON THE SUBJECT!
BOY! ALL I HAFTA DO IS LEARN HOW TO PREVENT BEIN' HYPNOTIZED AND I'VE GOT HIM!
...MMM-MUMBLE..."STARE FIXEDLY AT THE SUBJECT AND IN A LOW, STEADY VOICE SAY, 'SLEEP...SLEEP'..."
NO, THAT'S NOT IT!
"...AND IF PRACTISED FAITHFULLY, CANNOT FAIL! THE SUBJECT WILL BELIEVE HIMSELF A RABBIT OR..."
AW, PHOOEY!
EVERY ONE THE SAME! NOT A WORD FROM THE RABBIT'S ANGLE!

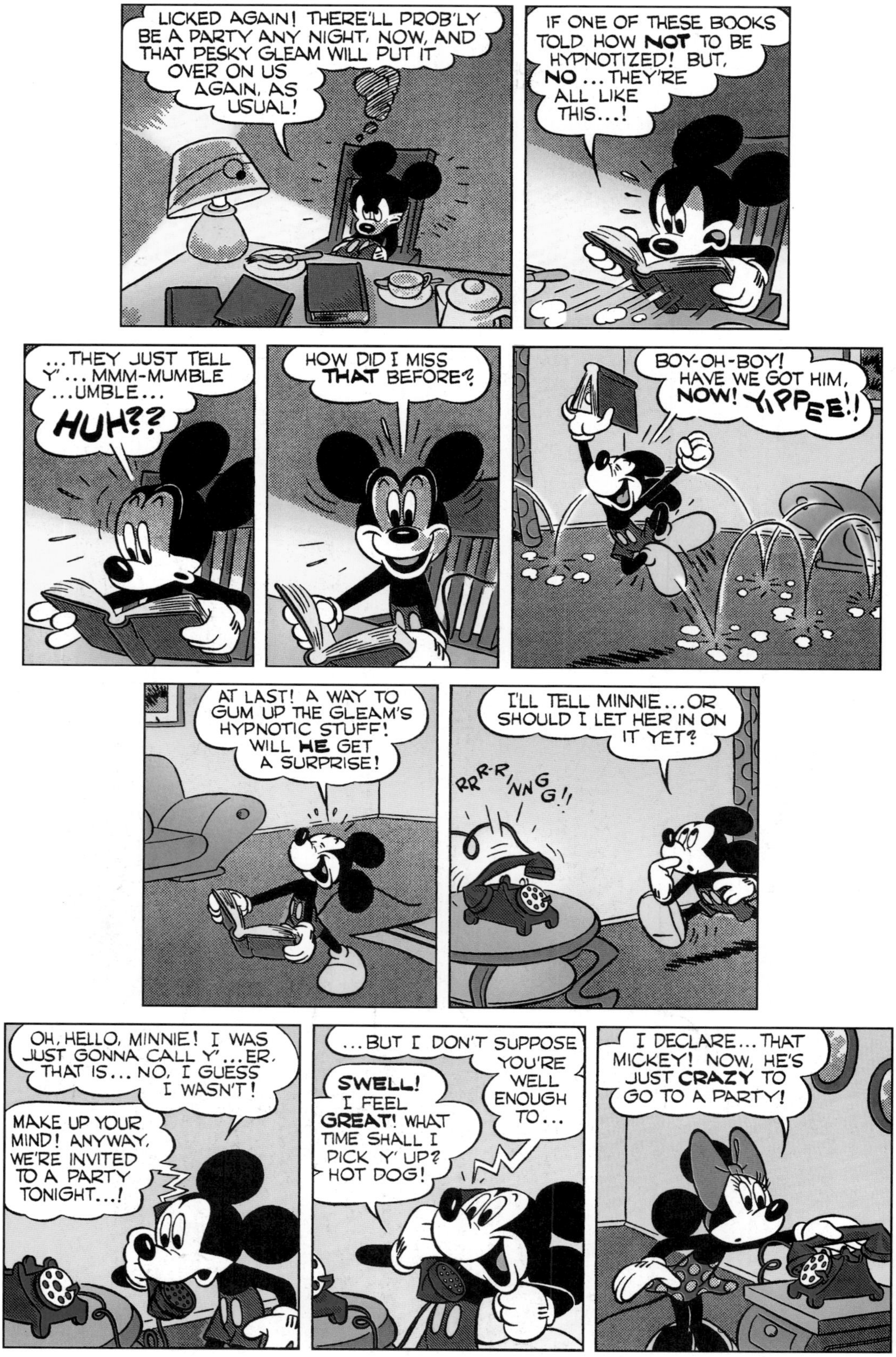
LICKED AGAIN! THERE'LL PROB'LY BE A PARTY ANY NIGHT, NOW, AND THAT PESKY GLEAM WILL PUT IT OVER ON US AGAIN, AS USUAL!
IF ONE OF THESE BOOKS TOLD HOW **NOT** TO BE HYPNOTIZED! BUT, **NO** ... THEY'RE ALL LIKE THIS...!
...THEY JUST TELL Y'... MMM-MUMBLE ...UMBLE...
HUH??
HOW DID I MISS **THAT** BEFORE?
BOY-OH-BOY! HAVE WE GOT HIM, **NOW**! YIPPEE!!
AT LAST! A WAY TO GUM UP THE GLEAM'S HYPNOTIC STUFF! WILL **HE** GET A SURPRISE!
RRR-RINNGG!!
I'LL TELL MINNIE...OR SHOULD I LET HER IN ON IT YET?
OH, HELLO, MINNIE! I WAS JUST GONNA CALL Y'...ER, THAT IS... NO, I GUESS I WASN'T!
MAKE UP YOUR MIND! ANYWAY, WE'RE INVITED TO A PARTY TONIGHT...!
...BUT I DON'T SUPPOSE YOU'RE WELL ENOUGH TO...
SWELL! I FEEL **GREAT**! WHAT TIME SHALL I PICK Y' UP? HOT DOG!
I DECLARE... THAT MICKEY! NOW, HE'S JUST **CRAZY** TO GO TO A PARTY!

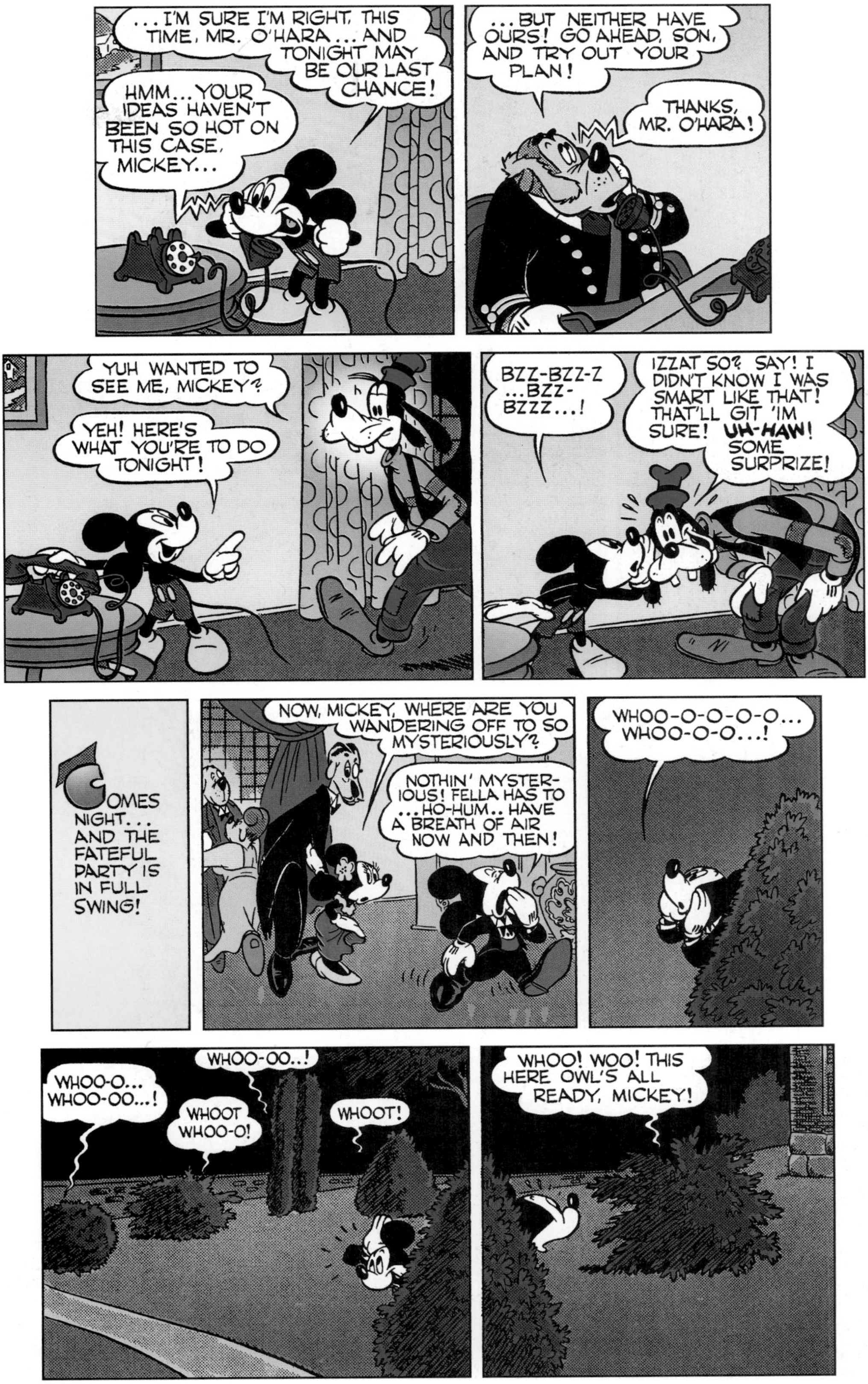
...I'M SURE I'M RIGHT THIS TIME, MR. O'HARA... AND TONIGHT MAY BE OUR LAST CHANCE!
HMM...YOUR IDEAS HAVEN'T BEEN SO HOT ON THIS CASE, MICKEY...
...BUT NEITHER HAVE OURS! GO AHEAD, SON, AND TRY OUT YOUR PLAN!
THANKS, MR. O'HARA!
YUH WANTED TO SEE ME, MICKEY?
YEH! HERE'S WHAT YOU'RE TO DO TONIGHT!
BZZ-BZZ-Z ...BZZ- BZZZ...!
IZZAT SO? SAY! I DIDN'T KNOW I WAS SMART LIKE THAT! THAT'LL GIT 'IM SURE! UH-HAW! SOME SURPRIZE!
COMES NIGHT... AND THE FATEFUL PARTY IS IN FULL SWING!
NOW, MICKEY, WHERE ARE YOU WANDERING OFF TO SO MYSTERIOUSLY?
NOTHIN' MYSTERIOUS! FELLA HAS TO ...HO-HUM.. HAVE A BREATH OF AIR NOW AND THEN!
WHOO-O-O-O-O... WHOO-O-O...!
WHOO-O... WHOO-OO...!
WHOO-OO..!
WHOOT WHOO-O!
WHOOT!
WHOO! WOO! THIS HERE OWL'S ALL READY, MICKEY!

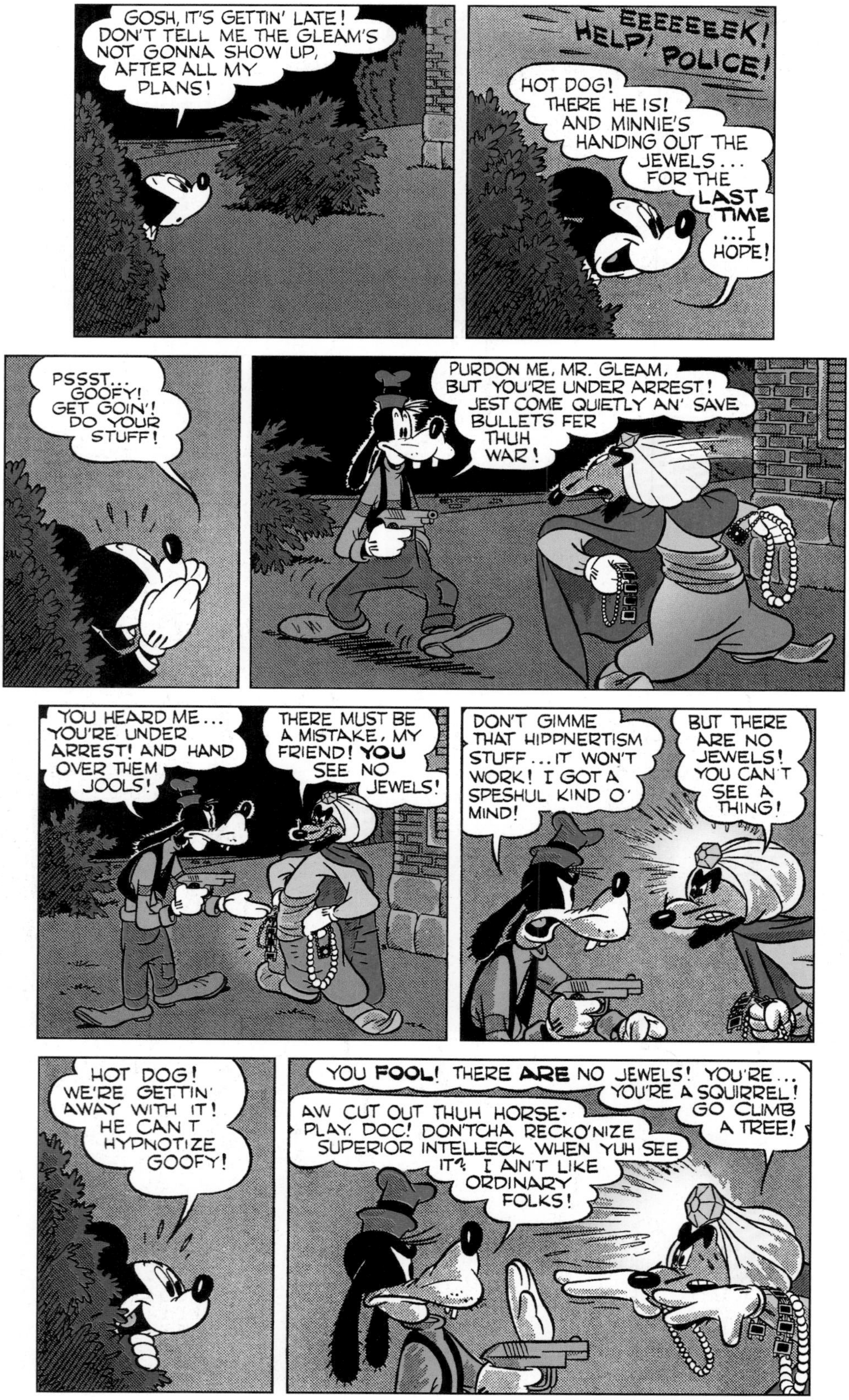
GOSH, IT'S GETTIN' LATE! DON'T TELL ME THE GLEAM'S NOT GONNA SHOW UP, AFTER ALL MY PLANS!
EEEEEEEK! HELP! POLICE!
HOT DOG! THERE HE IS! AND MINNIE'S HANDING OUT THE JEWELS... FOR THE LAST TIME ...I HOPE!
PSSST... GOOFY! GET GOIN'! DO YOUR STUFF!
PURDON ME, MR. GLEAM, BUT YOU'RE UNDER ARREST! JEST COME QUIETLY AN' SAVE BULLETS FER THUH WAR!
YOU HEARD ME... YOU'RE UNDER ARREST! AND HAND OVER THEM JOOLS!
THERE MUST BE A MISTAKE, MY FRIEND! YOU SEE NO JEWELS!
DON'T GIMME THAT HIPPNERTISM STUFF... IT WON'T WORK! I GOT A SPESHUL KIND O' MIND!
BUT THERE ARE NO JEWELS! YOU CAN'T SEE A THING!
HOT DOG! WE'RE GETTIN' AWAY WITH IT! HE CAN'T HYPNOTIZE GOOFY!
YOU FOOL! THERE ARE NO JEWELS! YOU'RE... YOU'RE A SQUIRREL! GO CLIMB A TREE!
AW CUT OUT THUH HORSE-PLAY, DOC! DON'TCHA RECKO'NIZE SUPERIOR INTELLECK WHEN YUH SEE IT?! I AIN'T LIKE ORDINARY FOLKS!

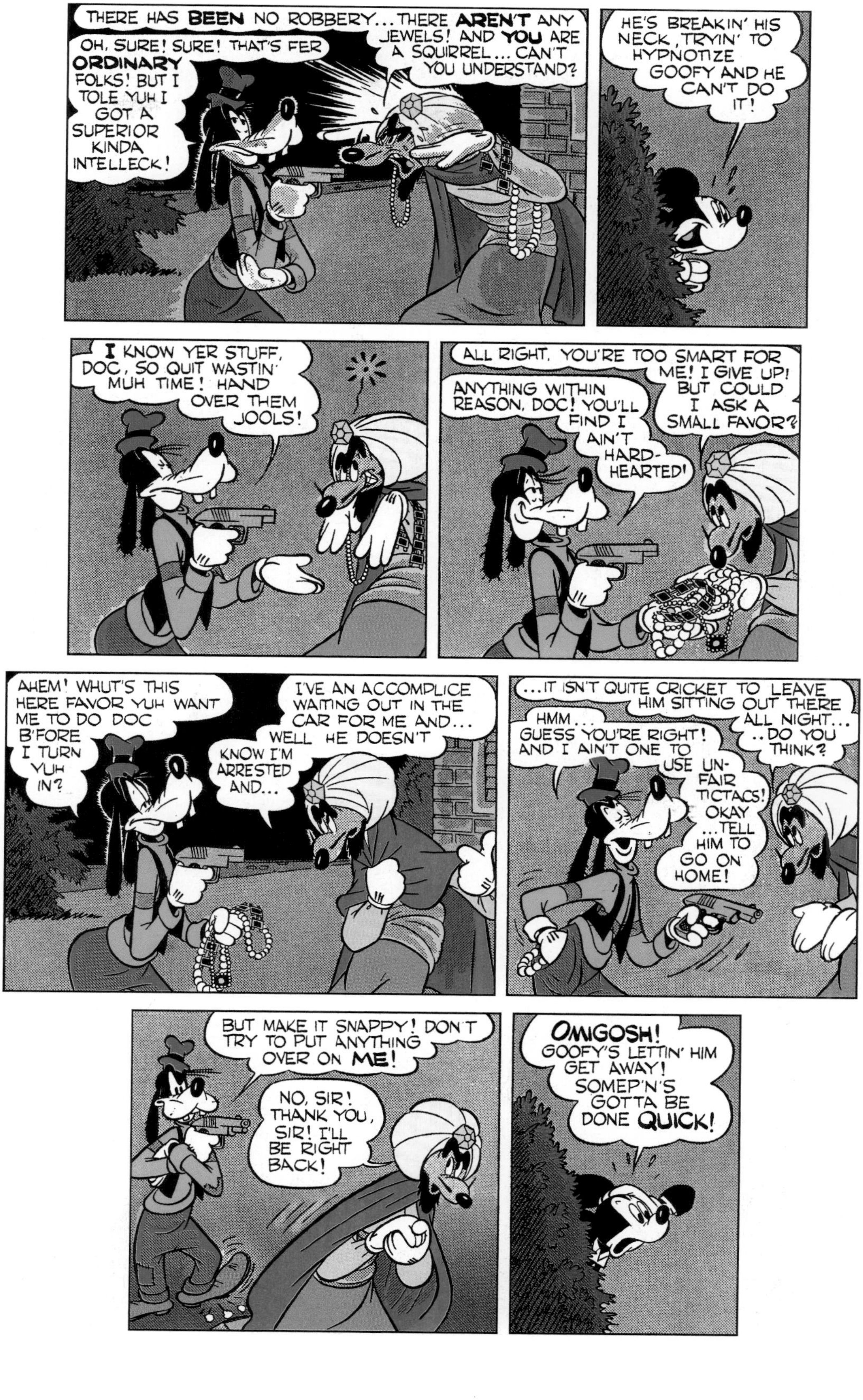
THERE HAS BEEN NO ROBBERY... THERE AREN'T ANY JEWELS! AND YOU ARE A SQUIRREL... CAN'T YOU UNDERSTAND?
OH, SURE! SURE! THAT'S FER ORDINARY FOLKS! BUT I TOLE YUH I GOT A SUPERIOR KINDA INTELLECK!
HE'S BREAKIN' HIS NECK, TRYIN' TO HYPNOTIZE GOOFY AND HE CAN'T DO IT!
I KNOW YER STUFF, DOC, SO QUIT WASTIN' MUH TIME! HAND OVER THEM JOOLS!
ALL RIGHT. YOU'RE TOO SMART FOR ME! I GIVE UP! BUT COULD I ASK A SMALL FAVOR?
ANYTHING WITHIN REASON, DOC! YOU'LL FIND I AIN'T HARD-HEARTED!
AHEM! WHUT'S THIS HERE FAVOR YUH WANT ME TO DO DOC B'FORE I TURN YUH IN?
I'VE AN ACCOMPLICE WAITING OUT IN THE CAR FOR ME AND... WELL HE DOESN'T KNOW I'M ARRESTED AND...
...IT ISN'T QUITE CRICKET TO LEAVE HIM SITTING OUT THERE ALL NIGHT... ..DO YOU THINK?
HMM... GUESS YOU'RE RIGHT! AND I AIN'T ONE TO USE UN-FAIR TICTACS! OKAY ...TELL HIM TO GO ON HOME!
BUT MAKE IT SNAPPY! DON'T TRY TO PUT ANYTHING OVER ON ME!
NO, SIR! THANK YOU, SIR! I'LL BE RIGHT BACK!
OMIGOSH! GOOFY'S LETTIN' HIM GET AWAY! SOMEP'N'S GOTTA BE DONE QUICK!

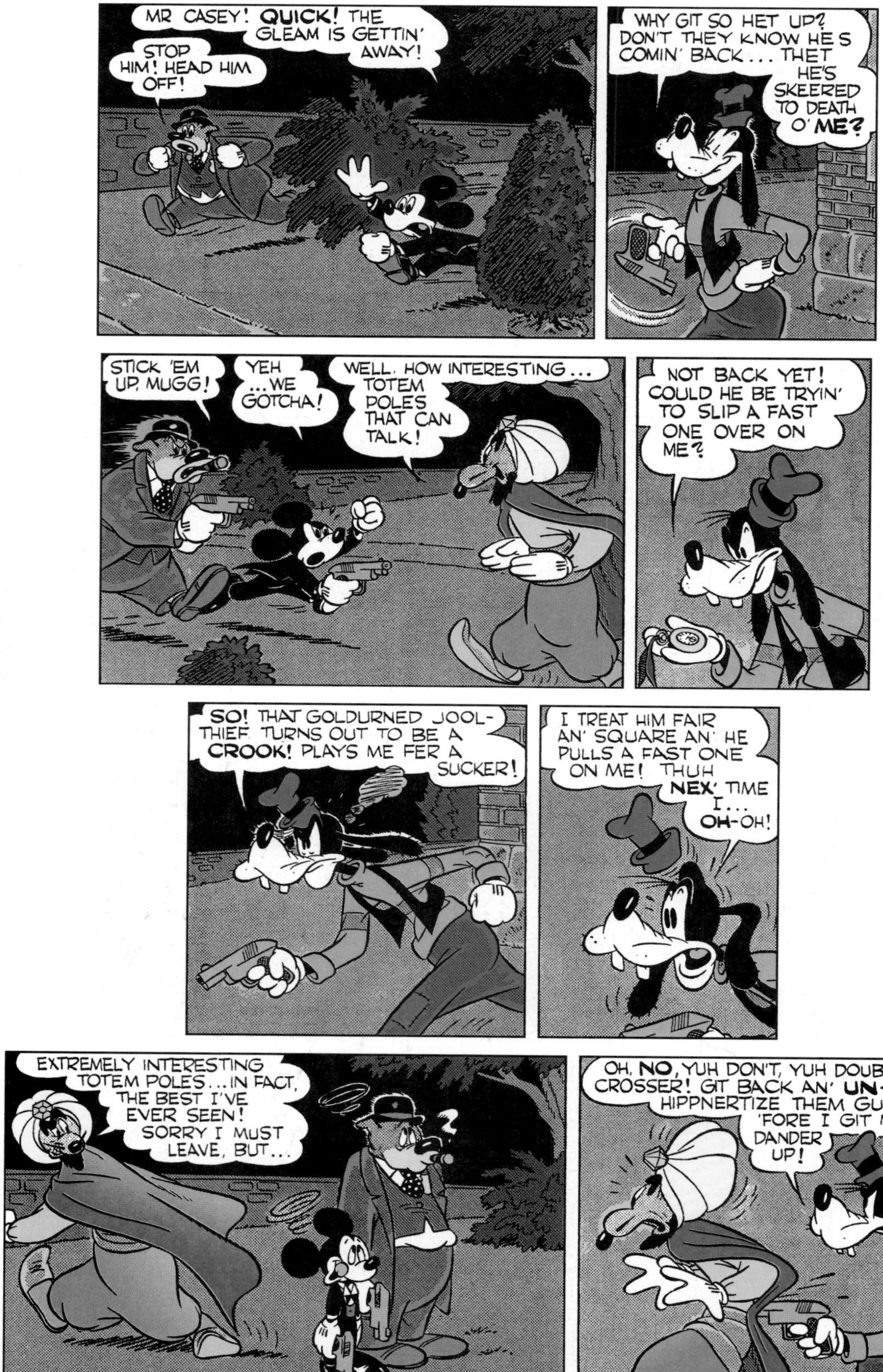
MR CASEY! QUICK! THE GLEAM IS GETTIN' AWAY!
STOP HIM! HEAD HIM OFF!
WHY GIT SO HET UP? DON'T THEY KNOW HE'S COMIN' BACK... THET HE'S SKEERED TO DEATH O' ME?
STICK 'EM UP, MUGG!
YEH ...WE GOTCHA!
WELL, HOW INTERESTING... TOTEM POLES THAT CAN TALK!
NOT BACK YET! COULD HE BE TRYIN' TO SLIP A FAST ONE OVER ON ME?
SO! THAT GOLDURNED JOOL-THIEF TURNS OUT TO BE A CROOK! PLAYS ME FER A SUCKER!
I TREAT HIM FAIR AN' SQUARE AN' HE PULLS A FAST ONE ON ME! THUH NEX' TIME I... OH-OH!
EXTREMELY INTERESTING TOTEM POLES... IN FACT, THE BEST I'VE EVER SEEN! SORRY I MUST LEAVE, BUT...
OH, NO, YUH DON'T, YUH DOUBLE-CROSSER! GIT BACK AN' UN-HIPPNERTIZE THEM GUYS, 'FORE I GIT MUH DANDER UP!

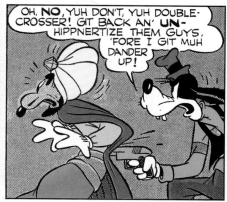

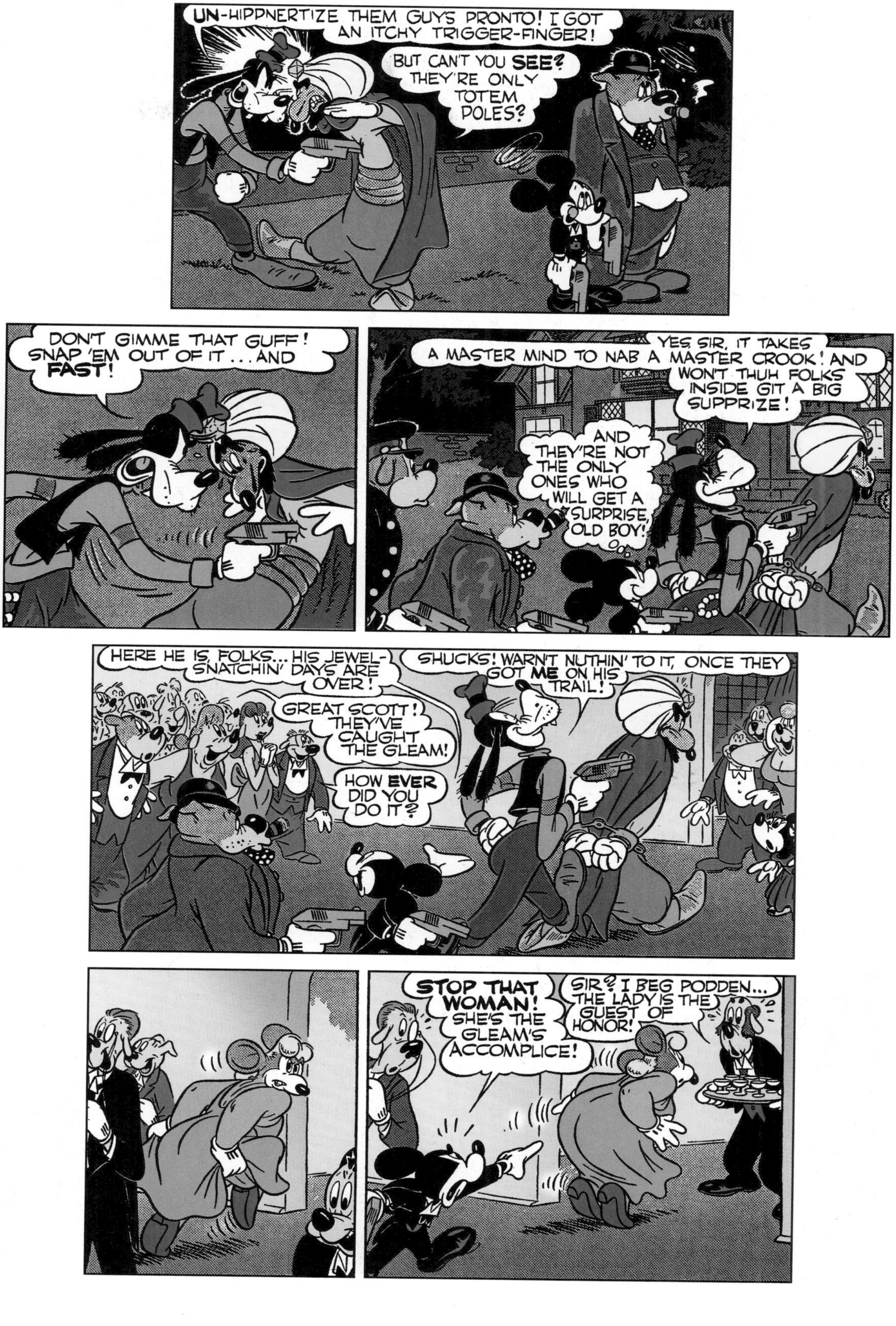
UN-HIPPNERTIZE THEM GUYS PRONTO! I GOT AN ITCHY TRIGGER-FINGER!
BUT CAN'T YOU SEE? THEY'RE ONLY TOTEM POLES?
DON'T GIMME THAT GUFF! SNAP 'EM OUT OF IT . . . AND FAST!
YES SIR, IT TAKES A MASTER MIND TO NAB A MASTER CROOK! AND WON'T THUH FOLKS INSIDE GIT A BIG SUPPRIZE!
AND THEY'RE NOT THE ONLY ONES WHO WILL GET A SURPRISE, OLD BOY!
HERE HE IS, FOLKS... HIS JEWEL-SNATCHIN' DAYS ARE OVER!
SHUCKS! WARN'T NUTHIN' TO IT, ONCE THEY GOT ME ON HIS TRAIL!
GREAT SCOTT! THEY'VE CAUGHT THE GLEAM!
HOW EVER DID YOU DO IT?
STOP THAT WOMAN! SHE'S THE GLEAM'S ACCOMPLICE!
SIR? I BEG PODDEN... THE LADY IS THE GUEST OF HONOR!

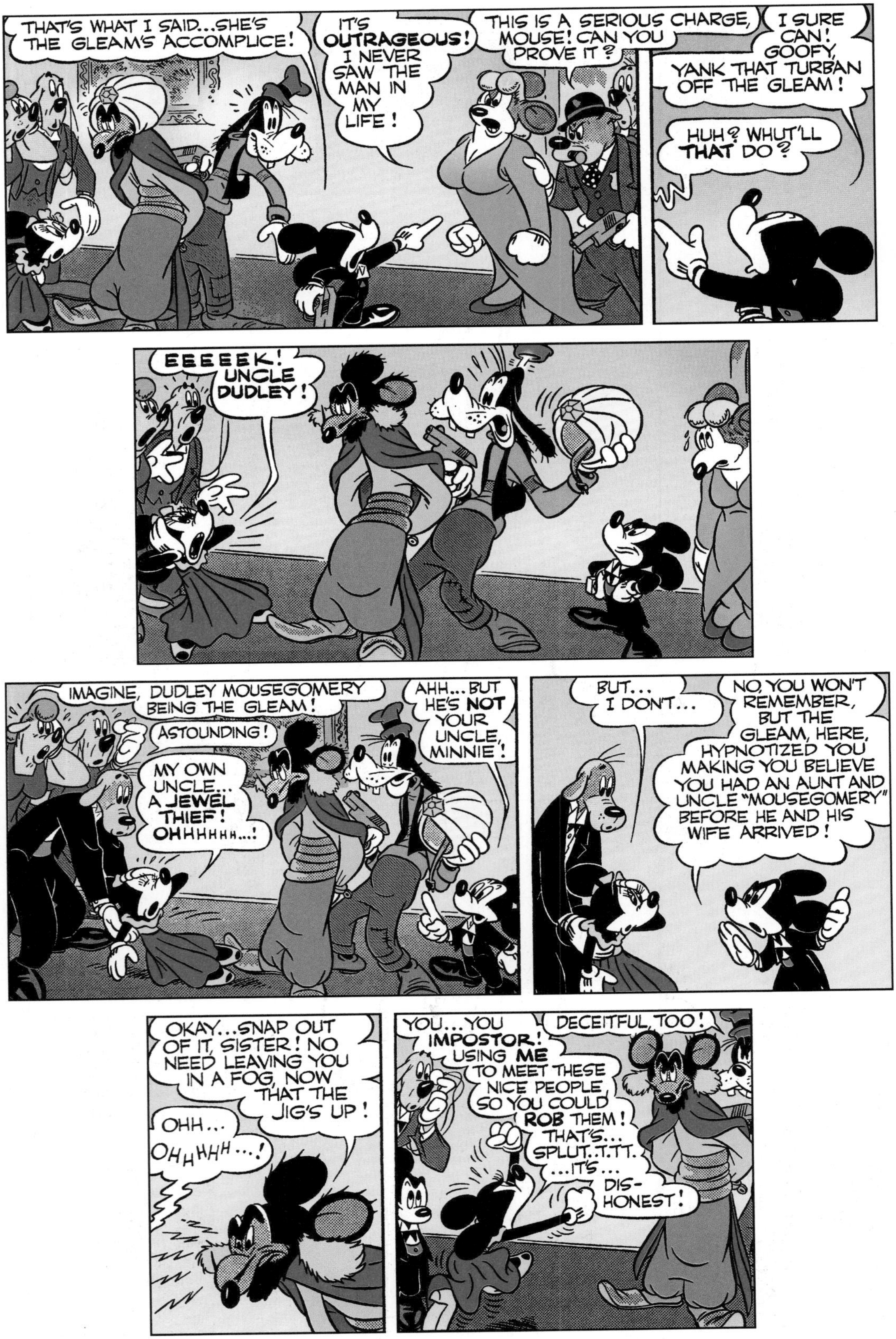
THAT'S WHAT I SAID...SHE'S THE GLEAM'S ACCOMPLICE!
IT'S OUTRAGEOUS! I NEVER SAW THE MAN IN MY LIFE!
THIS IS A SERIOUS CHARGE, MOUSE! CAN YOU PROVE IT?
I SURE CAN! GOOFY, YANK THAT TURBAN OFF THE GLEAM!
HUH? WHUT'LL THAT DO?
EEEEEK! UNCLE DUDLEY!
IMAGINE, DUDLEY MOUSEGOMERY BEING THE GLEAM!
ASTOUNDING!
MY OWN UNCLE... A JEWEL THIEF! OHHHHHH...!
AHH... BUT HE'S NOT YOUR UNCLE, MINNIE!
BUT... I DON'T...
NO, YOU WON'T REMEMBER, BUT THE GLEAM, HERE, HYPNOTIZED YOU MAKING YOU BELIEVE YOU HAD AN AUNT AND UNCLE "MOUSEGOMERY" BEFORE HE AND HIS WIFE ARRIVED!
OKAY...SNAP OUT OF IT, SISTER! NO NEED LEAVING YOU IN A FOG, NOW THAT THE JIG'S UP!
OHH... OHHHHH...!
YOU... YOU IMPOSTOR! USING ME TO MEET THESE NICE PEOPLE, SO YOU COULD ROB THEM! THAT'S... SPLUT..T.TT. ...IT'S... DIS-HONEST!
DECEITFUL, TOO!

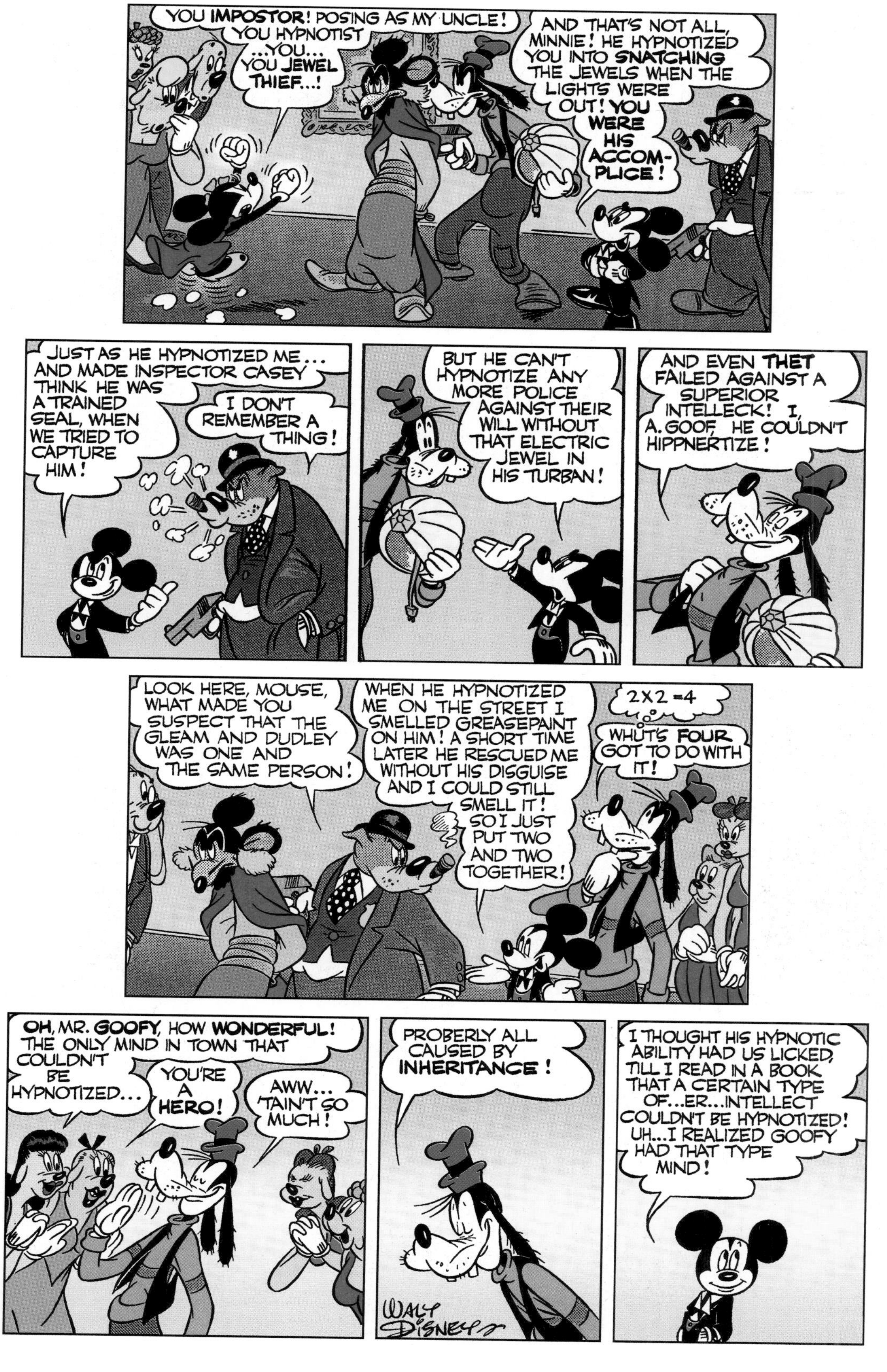

YOU IMPOSTOR! POSING AS MY UNCLE! YOU HYPNOTIST ...YOU... YOU JEWEL THIEF...!
AND THAT'S NOT ALL, MINNIE! HE HYPNOTIZED YOU INTO SNATCHING THE JEWELS WHEN THE LIGHTS WERE OUT! YOU WERE HIS ACCOMPLICE!
JUST AS HE HYPNOTIZED ME... AND MADE INSPECTOR CASEY THINK HE WAS A TRAINED SEAL, WHEN WE TRIED TO CAPTURE HIM!
I DON'T REMEMBER A THING!
BUT HE CAN'T HYPNOTIZE ANY MORE POLICE AGAINST THEIR WILL WITHOUT THAT ELECTRIC JEWEL IN HIS TURBAN!
AND EVEN THET FAILED AGAINST A SUPERIOR INTELLECK! I, A. GOOF, HE COULDN'T HIPPNERTIZE!
LOOK HERE, MOUSE, WHAT MADE YOU SUSPECT THAT THE GLEAM AND DUDLEY WAS ONE AND THE SAME PERSON!
WHEN HE HYPNOTIZED ME ON THE STREET I SMELLED GREASEPAINT ON HIM! A SHORT TIME LATER HE RESCUED ME WITHOUT HIS DISGUISE AND I COULD STILL SMELL IT! SO I JUST PUT TWO AND TWO TOGETHER!
2X2 =4
WHUT'S FOUR GOT TO DO WITH IT!
OH, MR. GOOFY, HOW WONDERFUL! THE ONLY MIND IN TOWN THAT COULDN'T BE HYPNOTIZED...
YOU'RE A HERO!
AWW... 'TAIN'T SO MUCH!
PROBERLY ALL CAUSED BY INHERITANCE!
WALT DISNEY
I THOUGHT HIS HYPNOTIC ABILITY HAD US LICKED, TILL I READ IN A BOOK THAT A CERTAIN TYPE OF...ER...INTELLECT COULDN'T BE HYPNOTIZED! UH...I REALIZED GOOFY HAD THAT TYPE MIND!

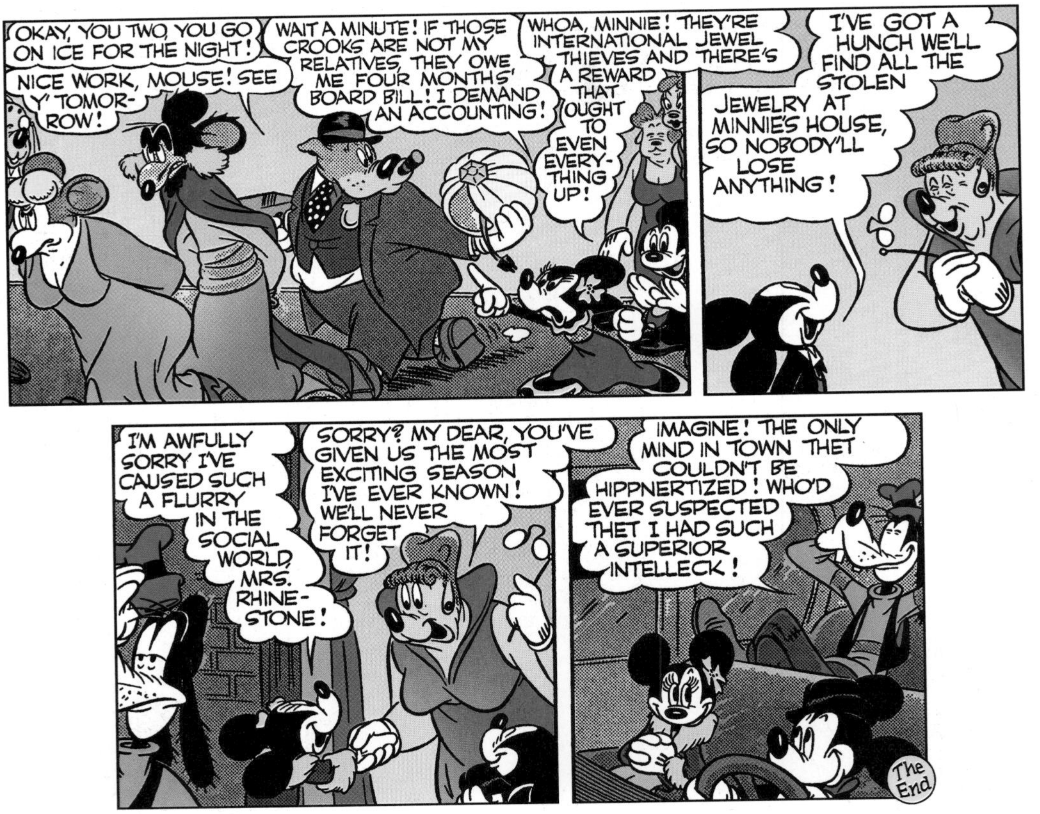
OKAY, YOU TWO, YOU GO ON ICE FOR THE NIGHT!
NICE WORK, MOUSE! SEE Y' TOMOR-ROW!
WAIT A MINUTE! IF THOSE CROOKS ARE NOT MY RELATIVES, THEY OWE ME FOUR MONTHS' BOARD BILL! I DEMAND AN ACCOUNTING!
WHOA, MINNIE! THEY'RE INTERNATIONAL JEWEL THIEVES AND THERE'S A REWARD THAT OUGHT TO EVEN EVERY-THING UP!
I'VE GOT A HUNCH WE'LL FIND ALL THE STOLEN JEWELRY AT MINNIE'S HOUSE, SO NOBODY'LL LOSE ANYTHING!
I'M AWFULLY SORRY I'VE CAUSED SUCH A FLURRY IN THE SOCIAL WORLD, MRS. RHINE-STONE!
SORRY? MY DEAR, YOU'VE GIVEN US THE MOST EXCITING SEASON I'VE EVER KNOWN! WE'LL NEVER FORGET IT!
IMAGINE! THE ONLY MIND IN TOWN THET COULDN'T BE HIPPNERTIZED! WHO'D EVER SUSPECTED THET I HAD SUCH A SUPERIOR INTELLECK!
The End

Walt Disney's SCAMP

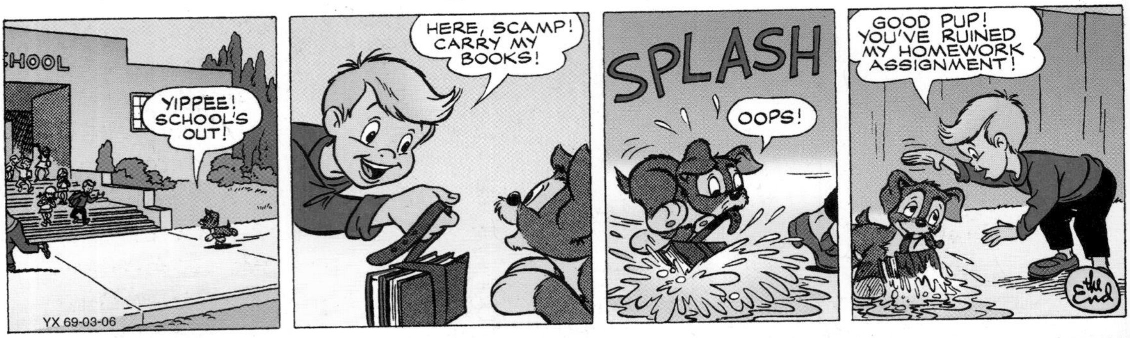
SCHOOL
YIPPEE! SCHOOL'S OUT!
YX 69-03-06
HERE, SCAMP! CARRY MY BOOKS!
SPLASH
OOPS!
GOOD PUP! YOU'VE RUINED MY HOMEWORK ASSIGNMENT!
the End

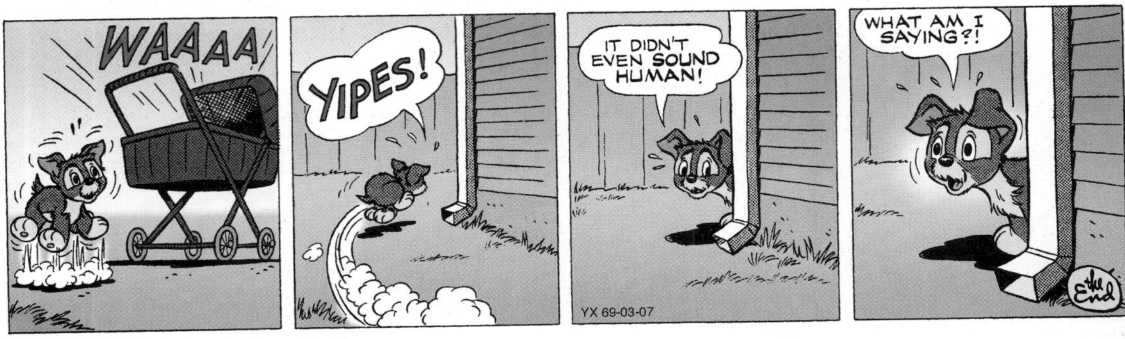
WAAAA
YIPES!
IT DIDN'T EVEN SOUND HUMAN!
YX 69-03-07
WHAT AM I SAYING?!
the End

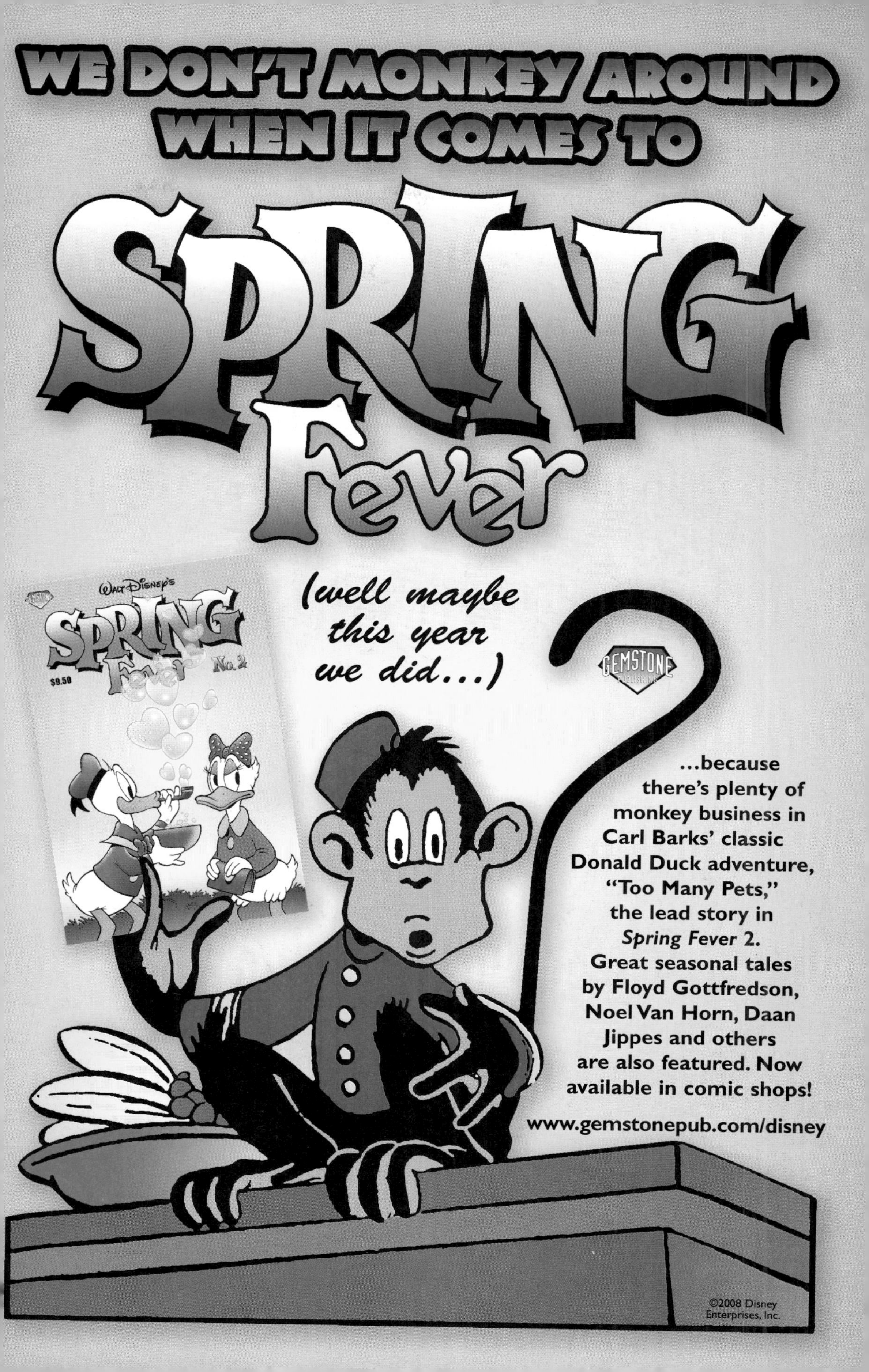
WE DON'T MONKEY AROUND WHEN IT COMES TO
SPRING Fever
(well maybe this year we did...)
GEMSTONE PUBLISHING
WALT DISNEY'S SPRING Fever No. 2
$9.50
...because there's plenty of monkey business in Carl Barks' classic Donald Duck adventure, "Too Many Pets," the lead story in Spring Fever 2. Great seasonal tales by Floyd Gottfredson, Noel Van Horn, Daan Jippes and others are also featured. Now available in comic shops!
www.gemstonepub.com/disney
©2008 Disney Enterprises, Inc.

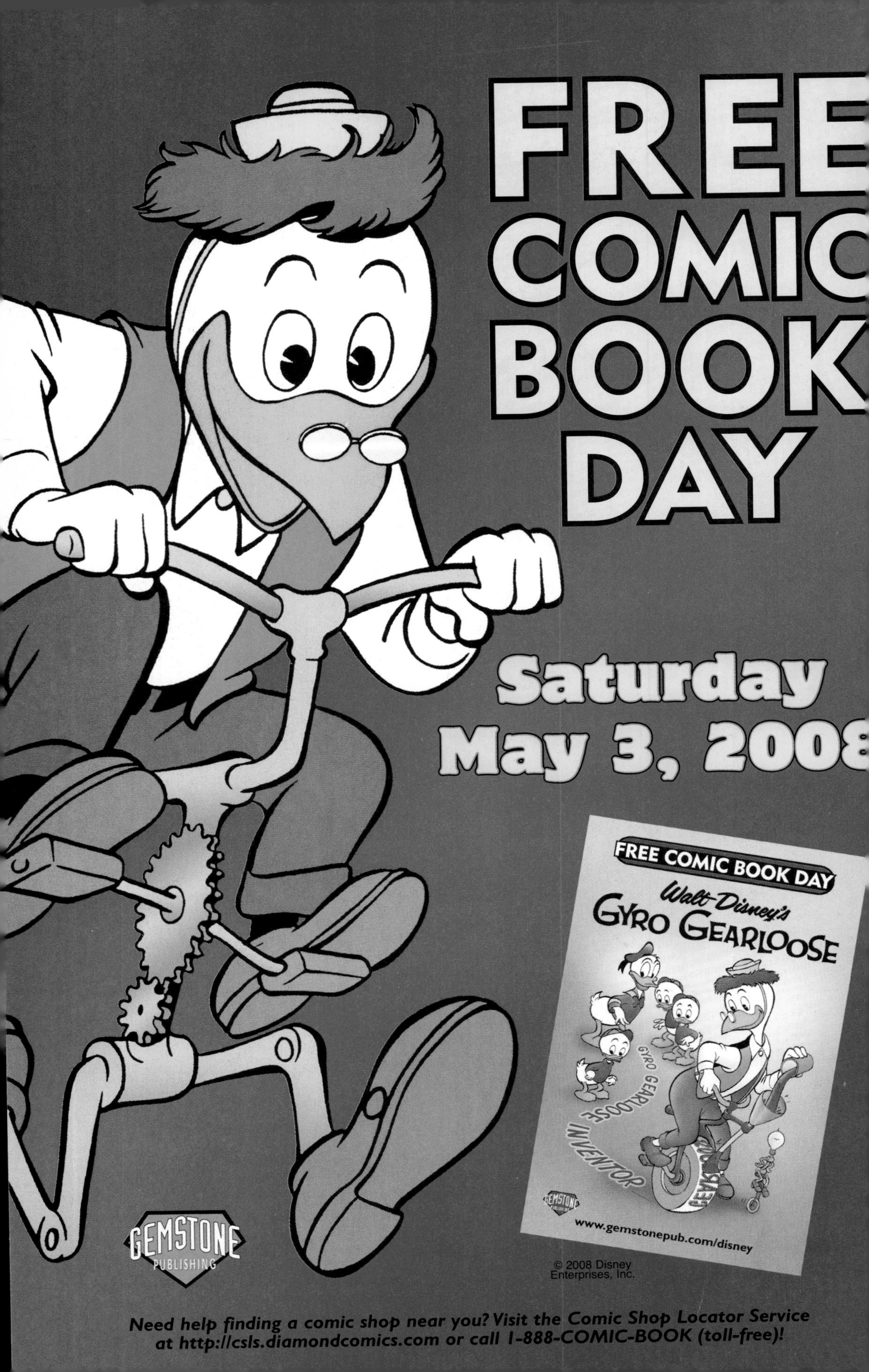
FREE COMIC BOOK DAY
Saturday May 3, 2008
FREE COMIC BOOK DAY
Walt Disney's
GYRO GEARLOOSE
GYRO GEARLOOSE INVENTOR
GEMSTONE PUBLISHING
www.gemstonepub.com/disney
© 2008 Disney Enterprises, Inc.
GEMSTONE PUBLISHING
Need help finding a comic shop near you? Visit the Comic Shop Locator Service at http://csls.diamondcomics.com or call 1-888-COMIC-BOOK (toll-free)!

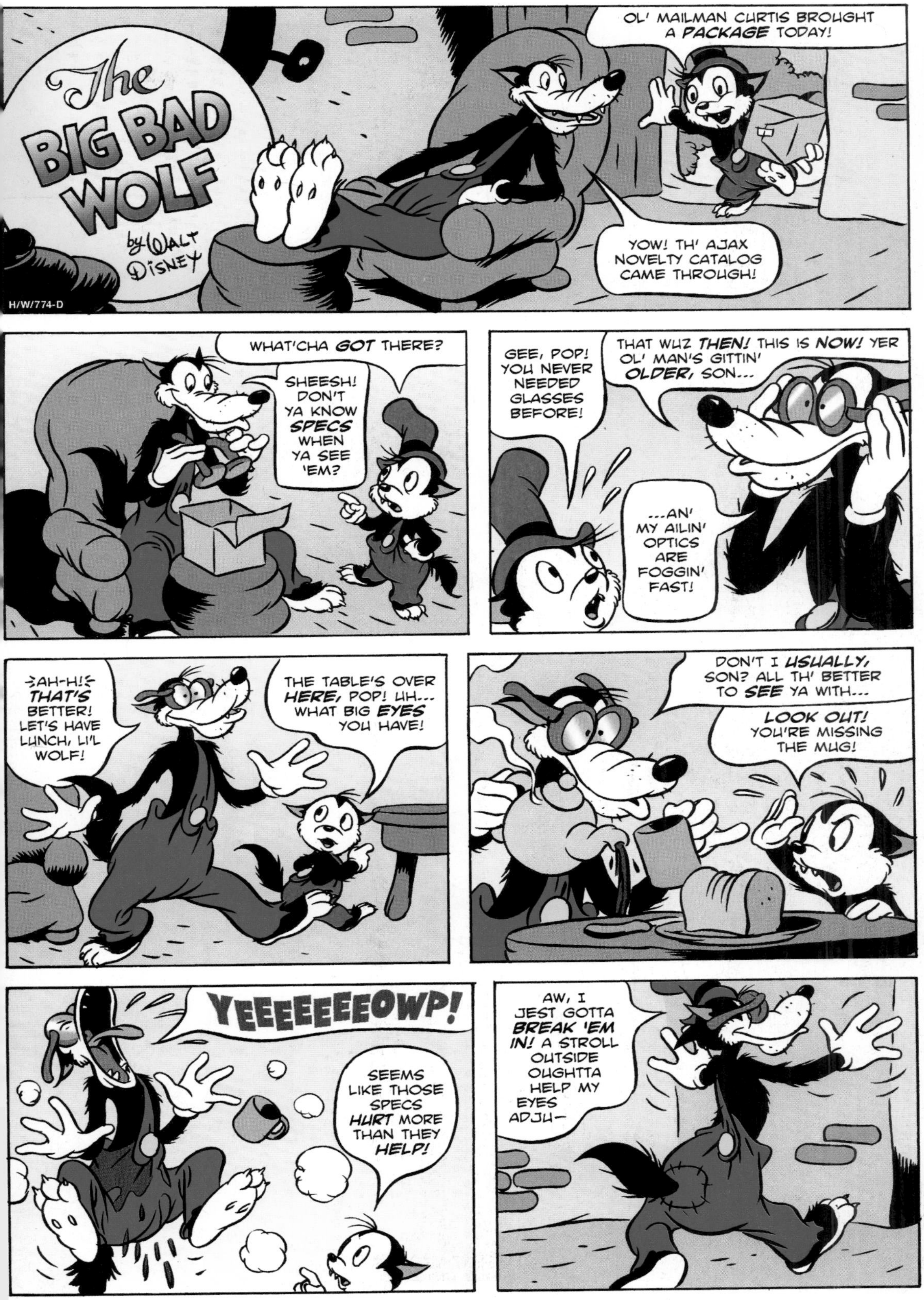
The BIG BAD WOLF
by WALT DISNEY
H/W/774-D
OL' MAILMAN CURTIS BROUGHT A PACKAGE TODAY!
YOW! TH' AJAX NOVELTY CATALOG CAME THROUGH!
WHAT'CHA GOT THERE?
SHEESH! DON'T YA KNOW SPECS WHEN YA SEE 'EM?
GEE, POP! YOU NEVER NEEDED GLASSES BEFORE!
THAT WUZ THEN! THIS IS NOW! YER OL' MAN'S GITTIN' OLDER, SON...
...AN' MY AILIN' OPTICS ARE FOGGIN' FAST!
AH-H! THAT'S BETTER! LET'S HAVE LUNCH, LI'L WOLF!
THE TABLE'S OVER HERE, POP! UH... WHAT BIG EYES YOU HAVE!
DON'T I USUALLY, SON? ALL TH' BETTER TO SEE YA WITH...
LOOK OUT! YOU'RE MISSING THE MUG!
YEEEEEEEOWP!
SEEMS LIKE THOSE SPECS HURT MORE THAN THEY HELP!
AW, I JEST GOTTA BREAK 'EM IN! A STROLL OUTSIDE OUGHTTA HELP MY EYES ADJU—

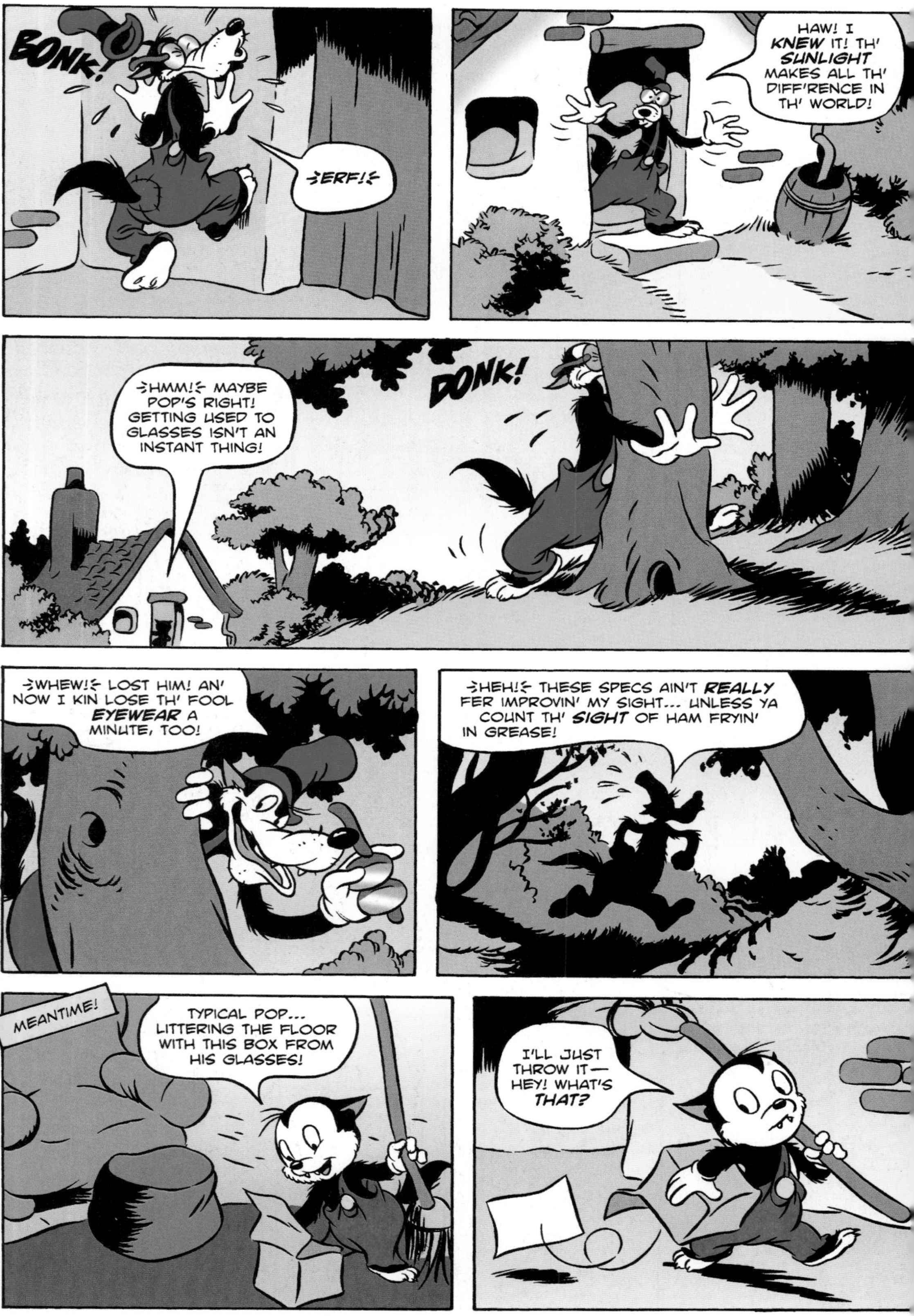
BONK!
ERF!
HAW! I KNEW IT! TH' SUNLIGHT MAKES ALL TH' DIFF'RENCE IN TH' WORLD!
HMM! MAYBE POP'S RIGHT! GETTING USED TO GLASSES ISN'T AN INSTANT THING!
DONK!
WHEW! LOST HIM! AN' NOW I KIN LOSE TH' FOOL EYEWEAR A MINUTE, TOO!
HEH! THESE SPECS AIN'T REALLY FER IMPROVIN' MY SIGHT... UNLESS YA COUNT TH' SIGHT OF HAM FRYIN' IN GREASE!
MEANTIME!
TYPICAL POP... LITTERING THE FLOOR WITH THIS BOX FROM HIS GLASSES!
I'LL JUST THROW IT— HEY! WHAT'S THAT?

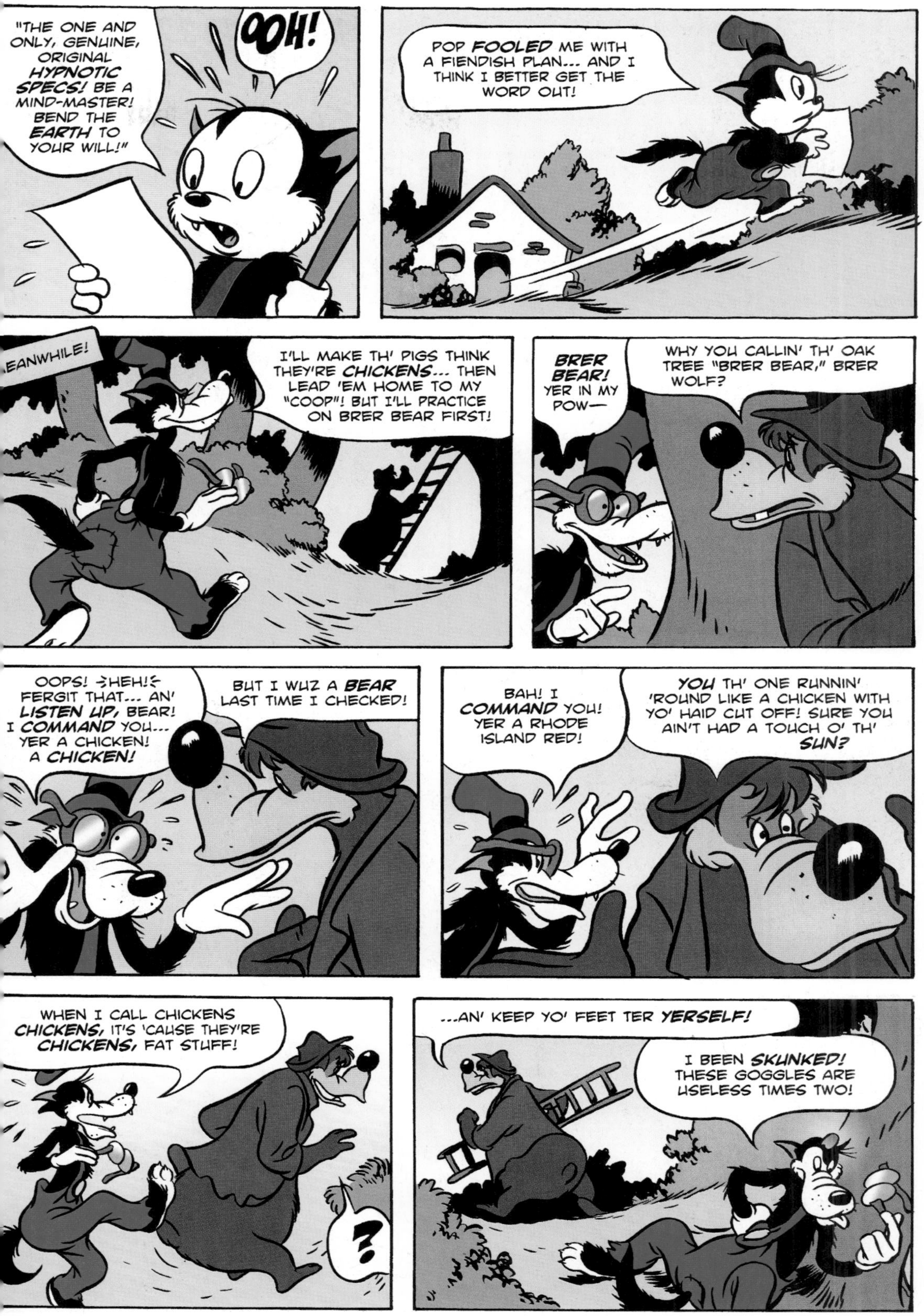
"THE ONE AND ONLY, GENUINE, ORIGINAL HYPNOTIC SPECS! BE A MIND-MASTER! BEND THE EARTH TO YOUR WILL!"
OOH!
POP FOOLED ME WITH A FIENDISH PLAN... AND I THINK I BETTER GET THE WORD OUT!
EANWHILE!
I'LL MAKE TH' PIGS THINK THEY'RE CHICKENS... THEN LEAD 'EM HOME TO MY "COOP"! BUT I'LL PRACTICE ON BRER BEAR FIRST!
BRER BEAR! YER IN MY POW—
WHY YOU CALLIN' TH' OAK TREE "BRER BEAR," BRER WOLF?
OOPS! HEH! FERGIT THAT... AN' LISTEN UP, BEAR! I COMMAND YOU... YER A CHICKEN! A CHICKEN!
BUT I WUZ A BEAR LAST TIME I CHECKED!
BAH! I COMMAND YOU! YER A RHODE ISLAND RED!
YOU TH' ONE RUNNIN' 'ROUND LIKE A CHICKEN WITH YO' HAID CUT OFF! SURE YOU AIN'T HAD A TOUCH O' TH' SUN?
WHEN I CALL CHICKENS CHICKENS, IT'S 'CAUSE THEY'RE CHICKENS, FAT STUFF!
?
...AN' KEEP YO' FEET TER YERSELF!
I BEEN SKUNKED! THESE GOGGLES ARE USELESS TIMES TWO!

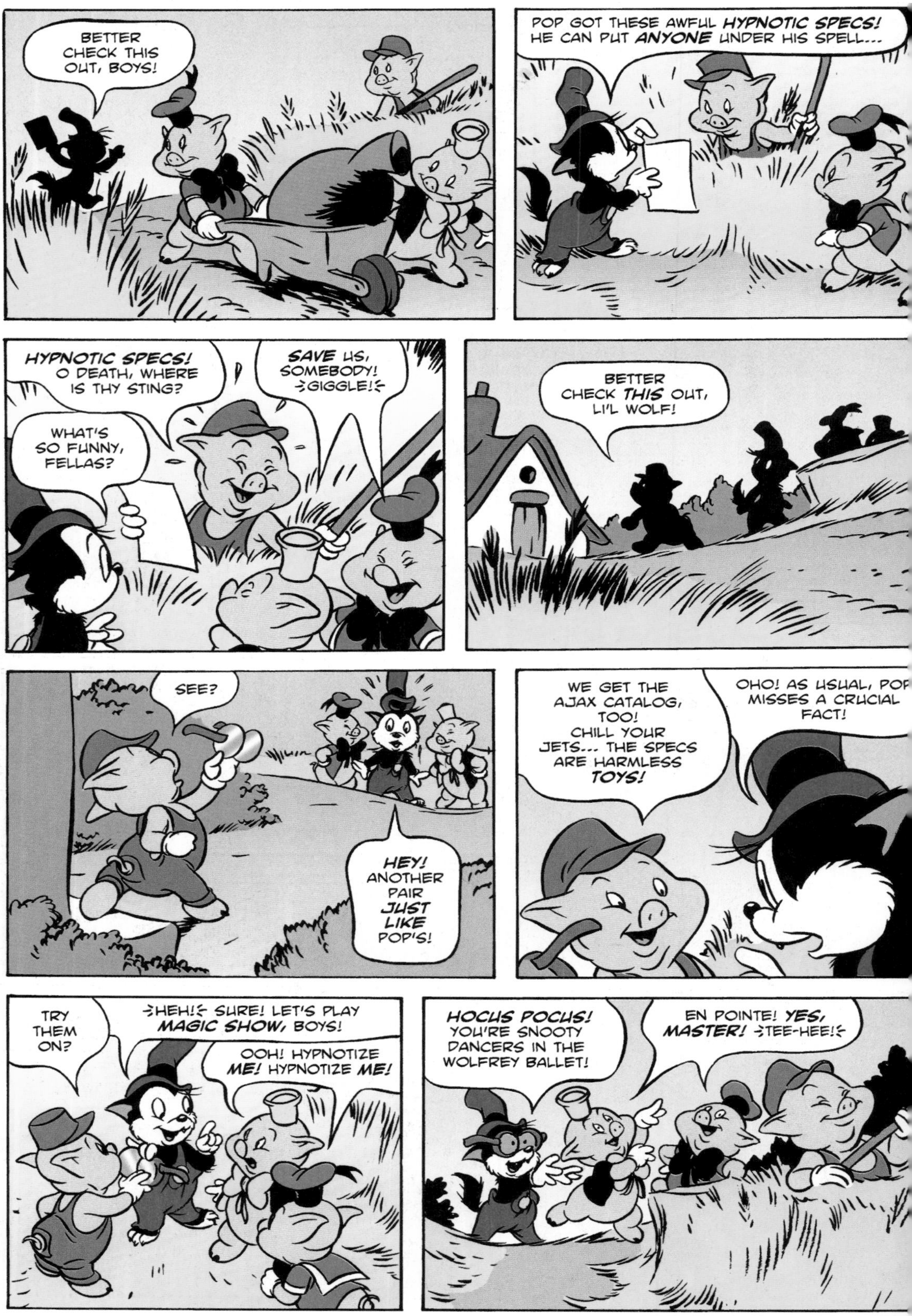
BETTER CHECK THIS OUT, BOYS!
POP GOT THESE AWFUL HYPNOTIC SPECS! HE CAN PUT ANYONE UNDER HIS SPELL...
HYPNOTIC SPECS! O DEATH, WHERE IS THY STING?
SAVE US, SOMEBODY! GIGGLE!
WHAT'S SO FUNNY, FELLAS?
BETTER CHECK THIS OUT, LI'L WOLF!
SEE?
HEY! ANOTHER PAIR JUST LIKE POP'S!
WE GET THE AJAX CATALOG, TOO! CHILL YOUR JETS... THE SPECS ARE HARMLESS TOYS!
OHO! AS USUAL, POP MISSES A CRUCIAL FACT!
TRY THEM ON?
HEH! SURE! LET'S PLAY MAGIC SHOW, BOYS!
OOH! HYPNOTIZE ME! HYPNOTIZE ME!
HOCUS POCUS! YOU'RE SNOOTY DANCERS IN THE WOLFREY BALLET!
EN POINTE! YES, MASTER! TEE-HEE!

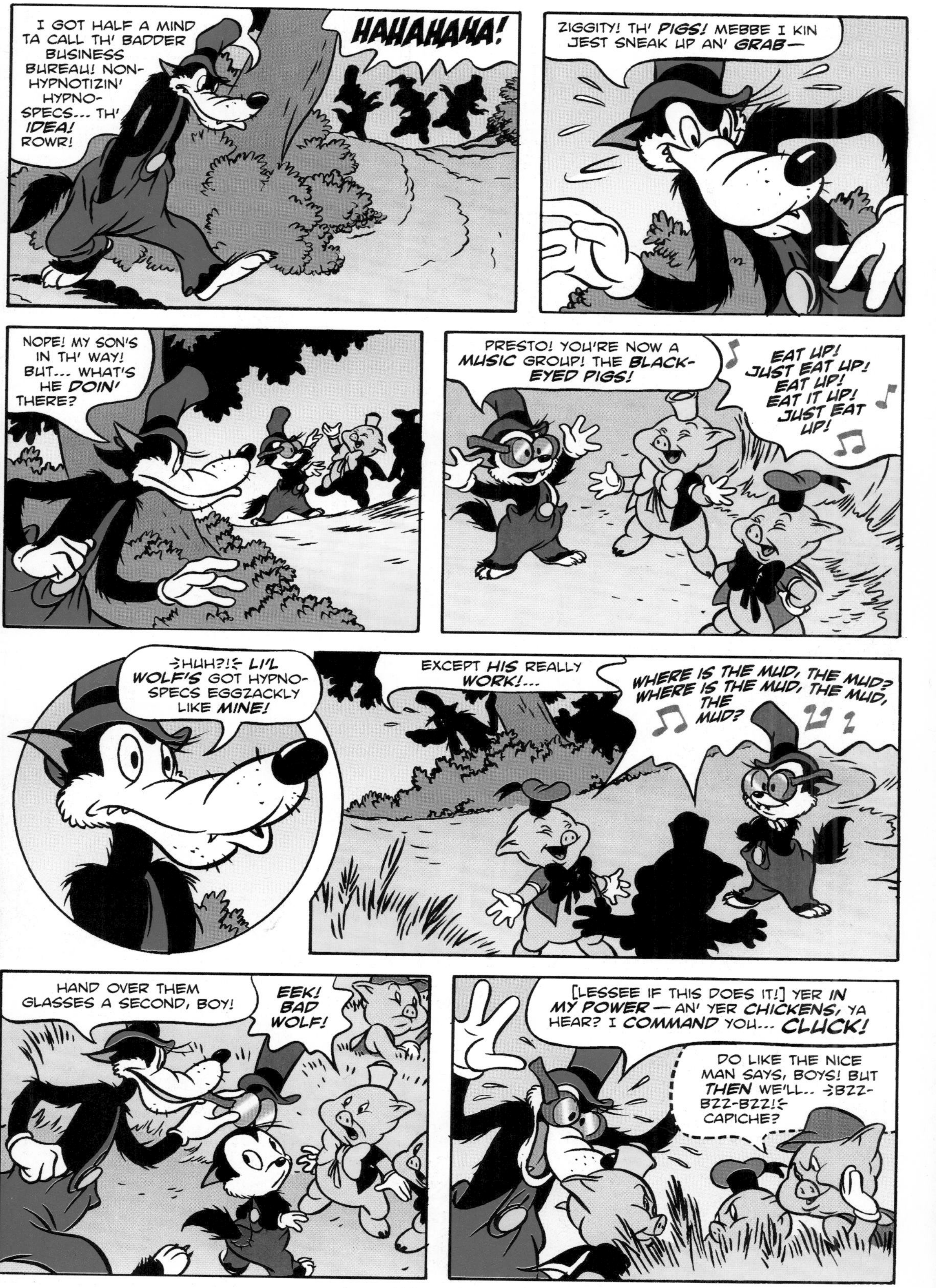
I GOT HALF A MIND TA CALL TH' BADDER BUSINESS BUREAU! NON-HYPNOTIZIN' HYPNO-SPECS... TH' IDEA! ROWR!
HAHAHAHA!
ZIGGITY! TH' PIGS! MEBBE I KIN JEST SNEAK UP AN' GRAB—
NOPE! MY SON'S IN TH' WAY! BUT... WHAT'S HE DOIN' THERE?
PRESTO! YOU'RE NOW A MUSIC GROUP! THE BLACK-EYED PIGS!
EAT UP! JUST EAT UP! EAT UP! EAT IT UP! JUST EAT UP!
HUH?! LI'L WOLF'S GOT HYPNO-SPECS EGGZACKLY LIKE MINE!
EXCEPT HIS REALLY WORK!...
WHERE IS THE MUD, THE MUD? WHERE IS THE MUD, THE MUD, THE MUD?
HAND OVER THEM GLASSES A SECOND, BOY!
EEK! BAD WOLF!
[LESSEE IF THIS DOES IT!] YER IN MY POWER — AN' YER CHICKENS, YA HEAR? I COMMAND YOU... CLUCK!
DO LIKE THE NICE MAN SAYS, BOYS! BUT THEN WE'LL... BZZ-BZZ-BZZ! CAPICHE?

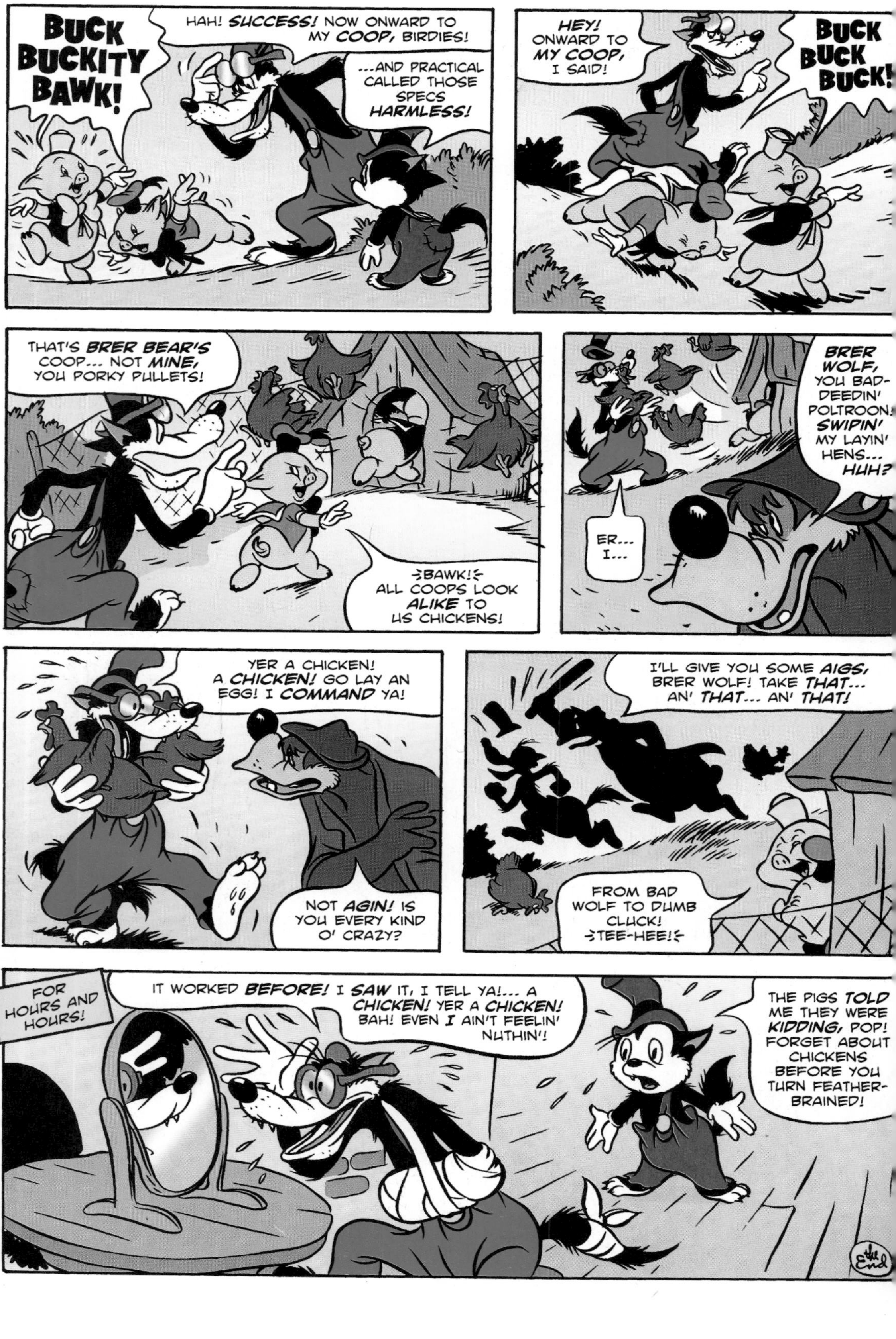

BUCK BUCKITY BAWK!
HAH! SUCCESS! NOW ONWARD TO MY COOP, BIRDIES!
...AND PRACTICAL CALLED THOSE SPECS HARMLESS!
HEY! ONWARD TO MY COOP, I SAID!
BUCK BUCK BUCK!
THAT'S BRER BEAR'S COOP... NOT MINE, YOU PORKY PULLETS!
BAWK! ALL COOPS LOOK ALIKE TO US CHICKENS!
BRER WOLF, YOU BAD-DEEDIN' POLTROON! SWIPIN' MY LAYIN' HENS... HUH?
ER... I...
YER A CHICKEN! A CHICKEN! GO LAY AN EGG! I COMMAND YA!
NOT AGIN! IS YOU EVERY KIND O' CRAZY?
I'LL GIVE YOU SOME AIGS, BRER WOLF! TAKE THAT... AN' THAT... AN' THAT!
FROM BAD WOLF TO DUMB CLUCK! TEE-HEE!
FOR HOURS AND HOURS!
IT WORKED BEFORE! I SAW IT, I TELL YA!... A CHICKEN! YER A CHICKEN! BAH! EVEN I AIN'T FEELIN' NUTHIN'!
THE PIGS TOLD ME THEY WERE KIDDING, POP! FORGET ABOUT CHICKENS BEFORE YOU TURN FEATHER-BRAINED!
the End

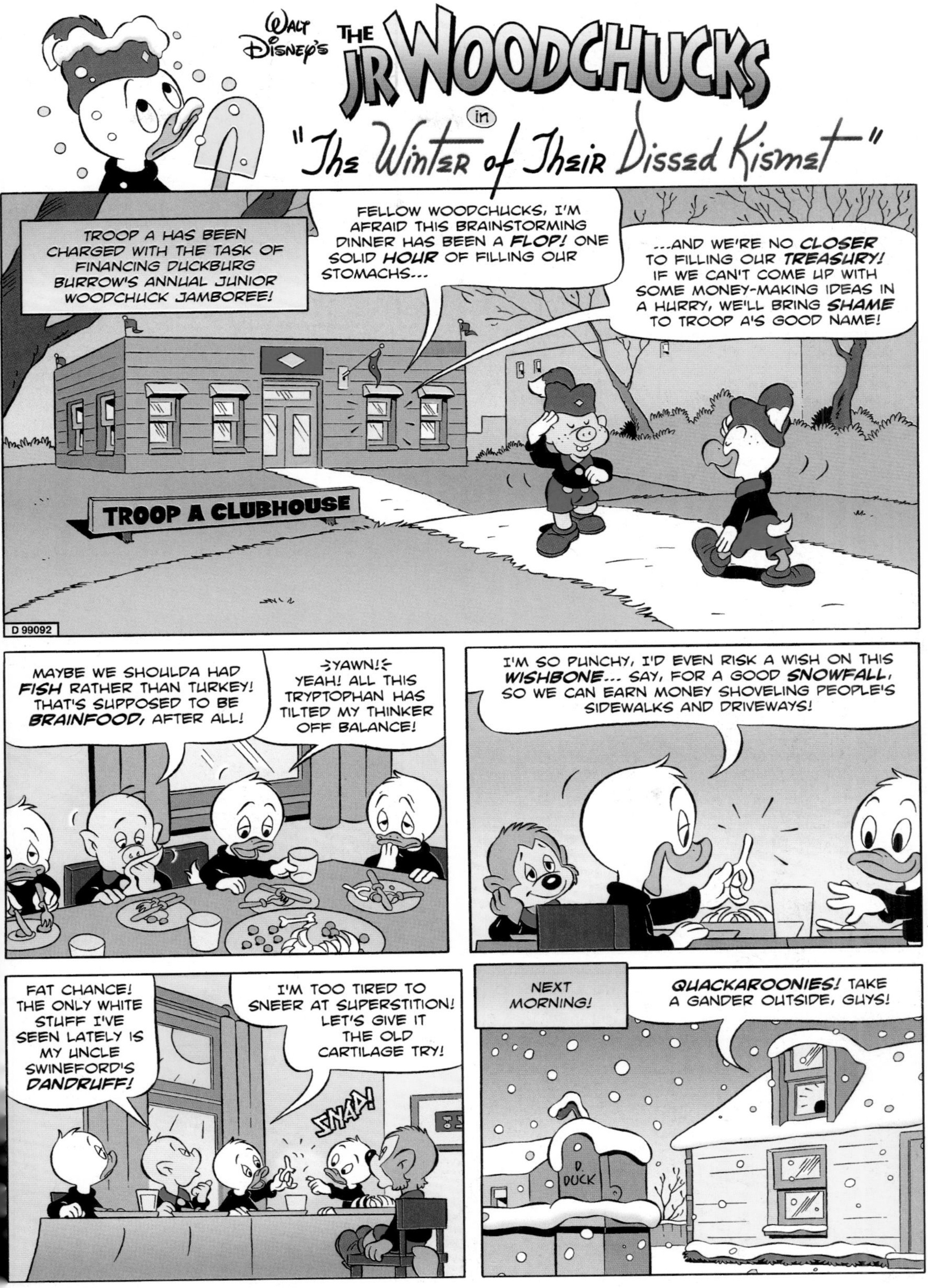
Walt Disney's
THE JR WOODCHUCKS
in
"The Winter of Their Dissed Kismet"
TROOP A HAS BEEN CHARGED WITH THE TASK OF FINANCING DUCKBURG BURROW'S ANNUAL JUNIOR WOODCHUCK JAMBOREE!
FELLOW WOODCHUCKS, I'M AFRAID THIS BRAINSTORMING DINNER HAS BEEN A FLOP! ONE SOLID HOUR OF FILLING OUR STOMACHS...
...AND WE'RE NO CLOSER TO FILLING OUR TREASURY! IF WE CAN'T COME UP WITH SOME MONEY-MAKING IDEAS IN A HURRY, WE'LL BRING SHAME TO TROOP A'S GOOD NAME!
TROOP A CLUBHOUSE
D 99092
MAYBE WE SHOULDA HAD FISH RATHER THAN TURKEY! THAT'S SUPPOSED TO BE BRAINFOOD, AFTER ALL!
YAWN! YEAH! ALL THIS TRYPTOPHAN HAS TILTED MY THINKER OFF BALANCE!
I'M SO PUNCHY, I'D EVEN RISK A WISH ON THIS WISHBONE... SAY, FOR A GOOD SNOWFALL, SO WE CAN EARN MONEY SHOVELING PEOPLE'S SIDEWALKS AND DRIVEWAYS!
FAT CHANCE! THE ONLY WHITE STUFF I'VE SEEN LATELY IS MY UNCLE SWINEFORD'S DANDRUFF!
I'M TOO TIRED TO SNEER AT SUPERSTITION! LET'S GIVE IT THE OLD CARTILAGE TRY!
SNAP!
NEXT MORNING!
QUACKAROONIES! TAKE A GANDER OUTSIDE, GUYS!
D. DUCK

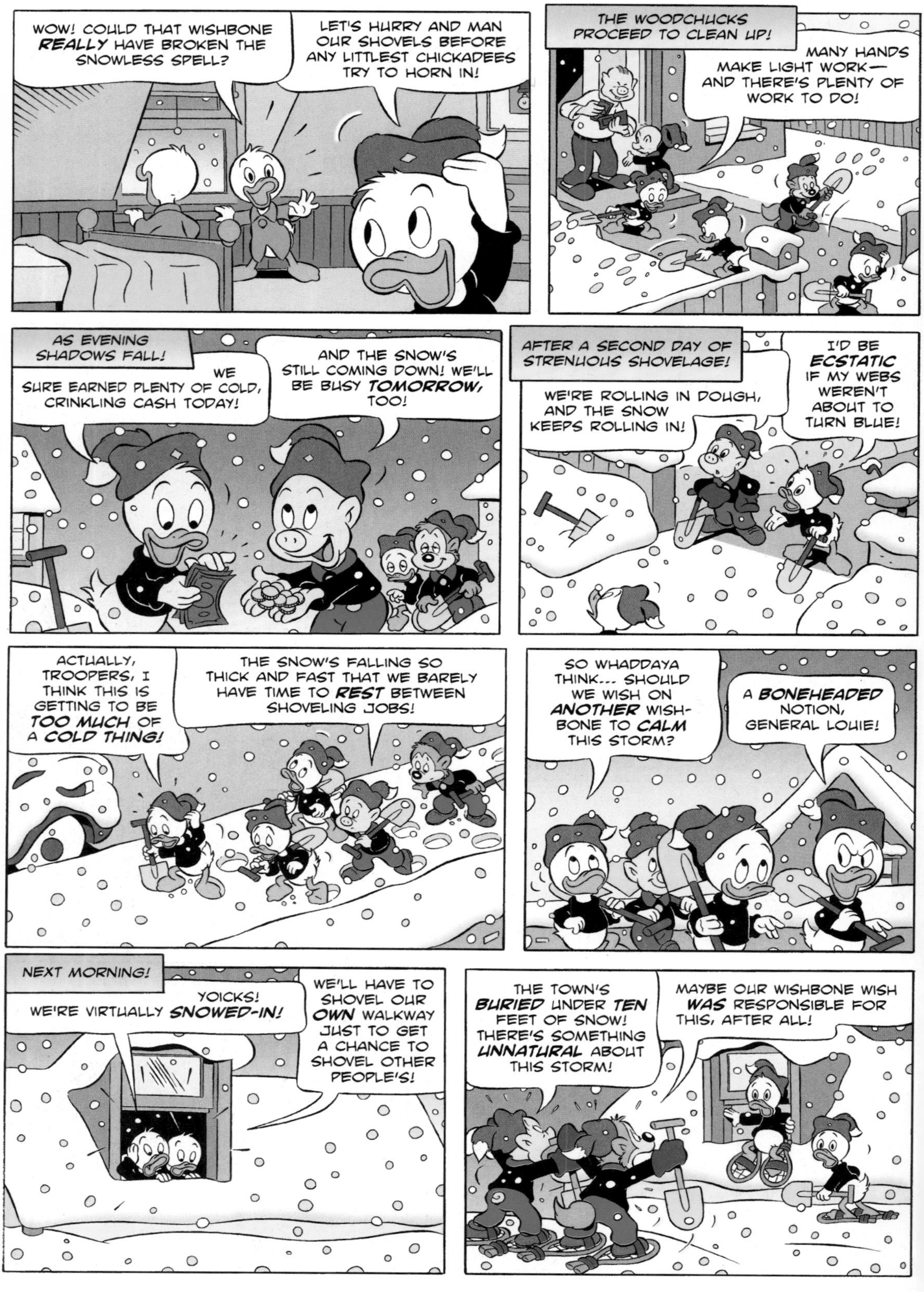
WOW! COULD THAT WISHBONE REALLY HAVE BROKEN THE SNOWLESS SPELL?
LET'S HURRY AND MAN OUR SHOVELS BEFORE ANY LITTLEST CHICKADEES TRY TO HORN IN!
THE WOODCHUCKS PROCEED TO CLEAN UP!
MANY HANDS MAKE LIGHT WORK— AND THERE'S PLENTY OF WORK TO DO!
AS EVENING SHADOWS FALL!
WE SURE EARNED PLENTY OF COLD, CRINKLING CASH TODAY!
AND THE SNOW'S STILL COMING DOWN! WE'LL BE BUSY TOMORROW, TOO!
AFTER A SECOND DAY OF STRENUOUS SHOVELAGE!
WE'RE ROLLING IN DOUGH, AND THE SNOW KEEPS ROLLING IN!
I'D BE ECSTATIC IF MY WEBS WEREN'T ABOUT TO TURN BLUE!
ACTUALLY, TROOPERS, I THINK THIS IS GETTING TO BE TOO MUCH OF A COLD THING!
THE SNOW'S FALLING SO THICK AND FAST THAT WE BARELY HAVE TIME TO REST BETWEEN SHOVELING JOBS!
SO WHADDAYA THINK... SHOULD WE WISH ON ANOTHER WISH-BONE TO CALM THIS STORM?
A BONEHEADED NOTION, GENERAL LOUIE!
NEXT MORNING!
YOICKS! WE'RE VIRTUALLY SNOWED-IN!
WE'LL HAVE TO SHOVEL OUR OWN WALKWAY JUST TO GET A CHANCE TO SHOVEL OTHER PEOPLE'S!
THE TOWN'S BURIED UNDER TEN FEET OF SNOW! THERE'S SOMETHING UNNATURAL ABOUT THIS STORM!
MAYBE OUR WISHBONE WISH WAS RESPONSIBLE FOR THIS, AFTER ALL!

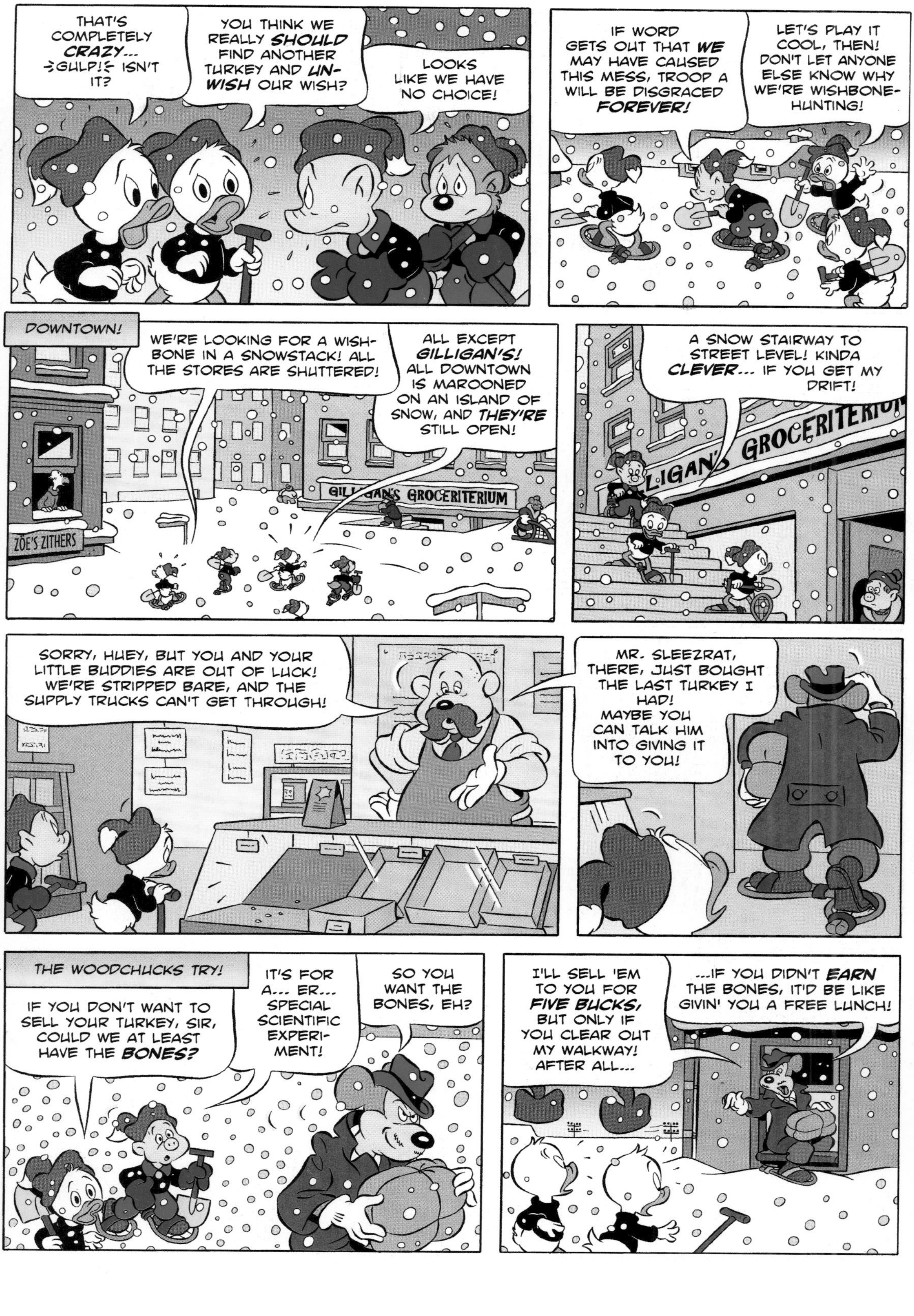
THAT'S COMPLETELY CRAZY... GULP! ISN'T IT?
YOU THINK WE REALLY SHOULD FIND ANOTHER TURKEY AND UN-WISH OUR WISH?
LOOKS LIKE WE HAVE NO CHOICE!
IF WORD GETS OUT THAT WE MAY HAVE CAUSED THIS MESS, TROOP A WILL BE DISGRACED FOREVER!
LET'S PLAY IT COOL, THEN! DON'T LET ANYONE ELSE KNOW WHY WE'RE WISHBONE-HUNTING!
DOWNTOWN!
WE'RE LOOKING FOR A WISH-BONE IN A SNOWSTACK! ALL THE STORES ARE SHUTTERED!
ALL EXCEPT GILLIGAN'S! ALL DOWNTOWN IS MAROONED ON AN ISLAND OF SNOW, AND THEY'RE STILL OPEN!
ZÖE'S ZITHERS
GILLIGAN'S GROCERITERIUM
A SNOW STAIRWAY TO STREET LEVEL! KINDA CLEVER... IF YOU GET MY DRIFT!
SORRY, HUEY, BUT YOU AND YOUR LITTLE BUDDIES ARE OUT OF LUCK! WE'RE STRIPPED BARE, AND THE SUPPLY TRUCKS CAN'T GET THROUGH!
MR. SLEEZRAT, THERE, JUST BOUGHT THE LAST TURKEY I HAD! MAYBE YOU CAN TALK HIM INTO GIVING IT TO YOU!
THE WOODCHUCKS TRY!
IF YOU DON'T WANT TO SELL YOUR TURKEY, SIR, COULD WE AT LEAST HAVE THE BONES?
IT'S FOR A... ER... SPECIAL SCIENTIFIC EXPERI-MENT!
SO YOU WANT THE BONES, EH?
I'LL SELL 'EM TO YOU FOR FIVE BUCKS, BUT ONLY IF YOU CLEAR OUT MY WALKWAY! AFTER ALL...
...IF YOU DIDN'T EARN THE BONES, IT'D BE LIKE GIVIN' YOU A FREE LUNCH!

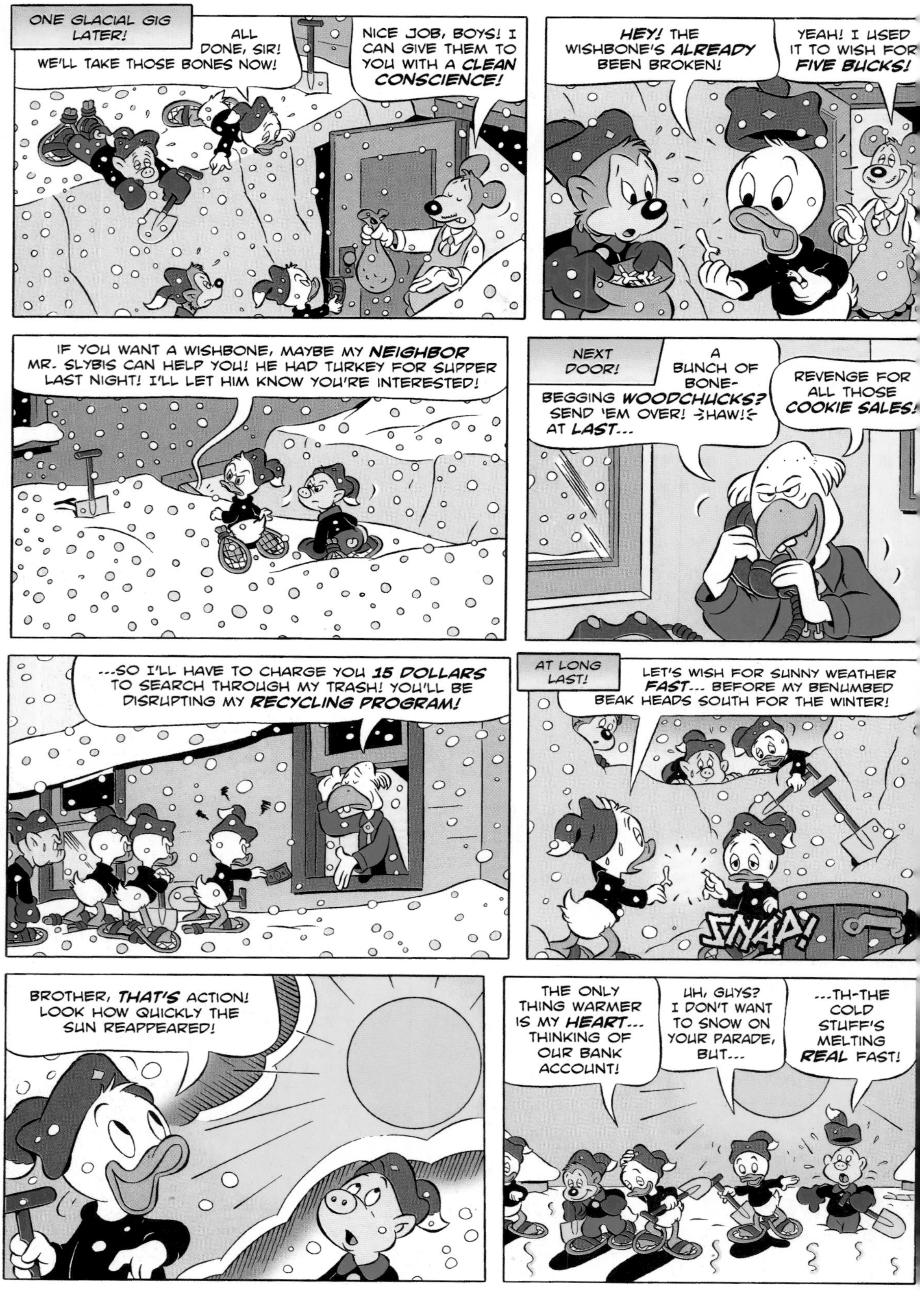
ONE GLACIAL GIG LATER!
ALL DONE, SIR! WE'LL TAKE THOSE BONES NOW!
NICE JOB, BOYS! I CAN GIVE THEM TO YOU WITH A CLEAN CONSCIENCE!
HEY! THE WISHBONE'S ALREADY BEEN BROKEN!
YEAH! I USED IT TO WISH FOR FIVE BUCKS!
IF YOU WANT A WISHBONE, MAYBE MY NEIGHBOR MR. SLYBIS CAN HELP YOU! HE HAD TURKEY FOR SUPPER LAST NIGHT! I'LL LET HIM KNOW YOU'RE INTERESTED!
NEXT DOOR!
A BUNCH OF BONE-BEGGING WOODCHUCKS? SEND 'EM OVER! HAW! AT LAST...
REVENGE FOR ALL THOSE COOKIE SALES!
...SO I'LL HAVE TO CHARGE YOU 15 DOLLARS TO SEARCH THROUGH MY TRASH! YOU'LL BE DISRUPTING MY RECYCLING PROGRAM!
AT LONG LAST!
LET'S WISH FOR SUNNY WEATHER FAST... BEFORE MY BENUMBED BEAK HEADS SOUTH FOR THE WINTER!
SNAP!
BROTHER, THAT'S ACTION! LOOK HOW QUICKLY THE SUN REAPPEARED!
THE ONLY THING WARMER IS MY HEART... THINKING OF OUR BANK ACCOUNT!
UH, GUYS? I DON'T WANT TO SNOW ON YOUR PARADE, BUT...
...TH-THE COLD STUFF'S MELTING REAL FAST!

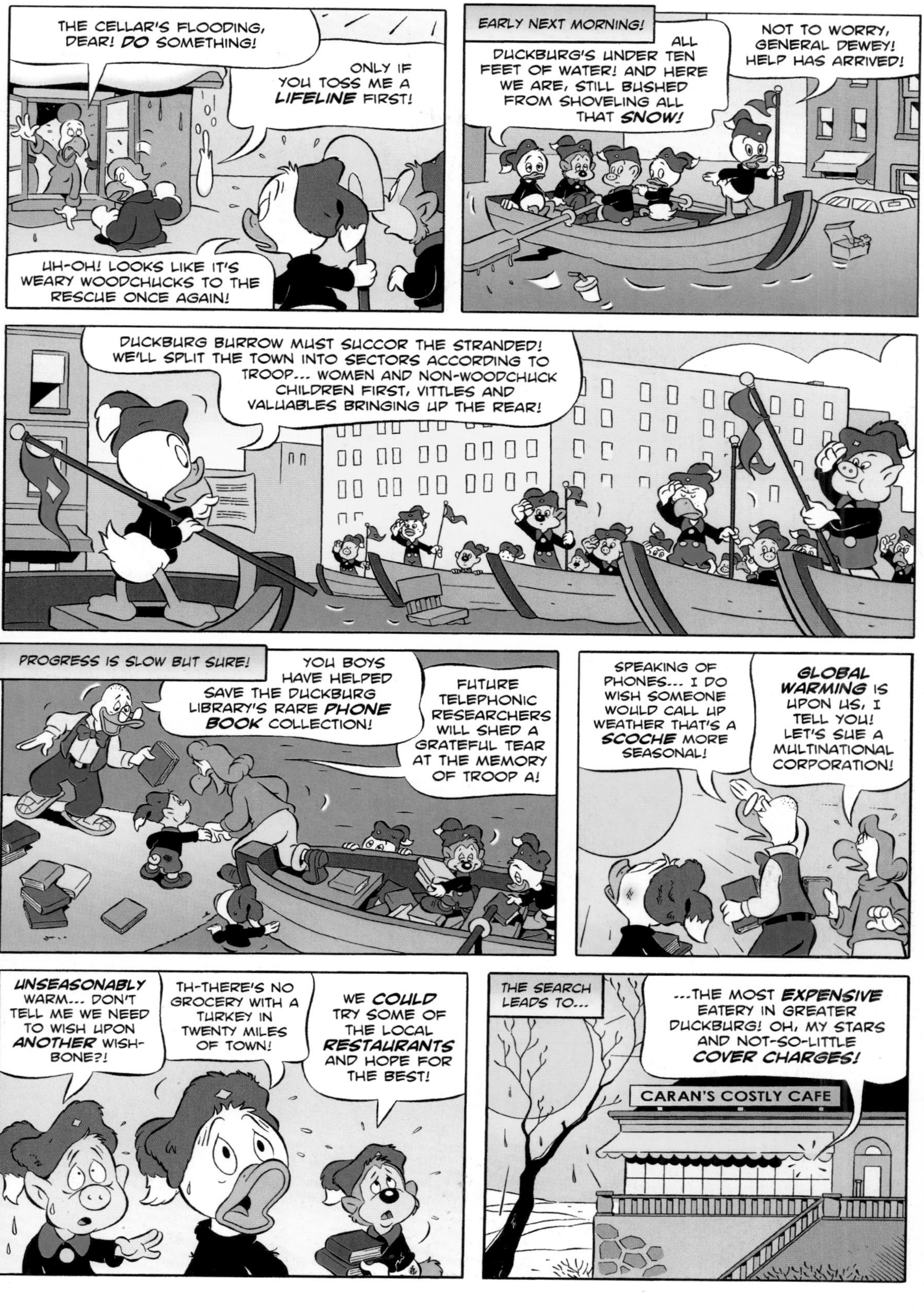
THE CELLAR'S FLOODING, DEAR! DO SOMETHING!
ONLY IF YOU TOSS ME A LIFELINE FIRST!
UH-OH! LOOKS LIKE IT'S WEARY WOODCHUCKS TO THE RESCUE ONCE AGAIN!
EARLY NEXT MORNING!
ALL DUCKBURG'S UNDER TEN FEET OF WATER! AND HERE WE ARE, STILL BUSHED FROM SHOVELING ALL THAT SNOW!
NOT TO WORRY, GENERAL DEWEY! HELP HAS ARRIVED!
DUCKBURG BURROW MUST SUCCOR THE STRANDED! WE'LL SPLIT THE TOWN INTO SECTORS ACCORDING TO TROOP... WOMEN AND NON-WOODCHUCK CHILDREN FIRST, VITTLES AND VALUABLES BRINGING UP THE REAR!
PROGRESS IS SLOW BUT SURE!
YOU BOYS HAVE HELPED SAVE THE DUCKBURG LIBRARY'S RARE PHONE BOOK COLLECTION!
FUTURE TELEPHONIC RESEARCHERS WILL SHED A GRATEFUL TEAR AT THE MEMORY OF TROOP A!
SPEAKING OF PHONES... I DO WISH SOMEONE WOULD CALL UP WEATHER THAT'S A SCOCHE MORE SEASONAL!
GLOBAL WARMING IS UPON US, I TELL YOU! LET'S SUE A MULTINATIONAL CORPORATION!
UNSEASONABLY WARM... DON'T TELL ME WE NEED TO WISH UPON ANOTHER WISH-BONE?!
TH-THERE'S NO GROCERY WITH A TURKEY IN TWENTY MILES OF TOWN!
WE COULD TRY SOME OF THE LOCAL RESTAURANTS AND HOPE FOR THE BEST!
THE SEARCH LEADS TO...
...THE MOST EXPENSIVE EATERY IN GREATER DUCKBURG! OH, MY STARS AND NOT-SO-LITTLE COVER CHARGES!
CARAN'S COSTLY CAFE

ONE TURKEY **WITHOUT** ALL THE TRIMMINGS WAS ENOUGH TO SIPHON OFF ALL OUR HARD-EARNED CASH!

THEY COULD AT LEAST HAVE GIVEN US SOME **BREAD-STICKS** TOO!

SHALL WE GET THIS OVER WITH?

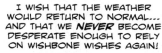

I WISH THAT THE WEATHER WOULD RETURN TO NORMAL.... AND THAT WE **NEVER** BECOME DESPERATE ENOUGH TO RELY ON WISHBONE WISHES AGAIN!

SNAP!

SUN'S STILL ABLAZE! THE WISH MUST HAVE WILTED, OR SOMETHING!

WHAT'RE WE GONNA DO **NOW?**

WORRIED ABOUT THE SUDDEN COLD AND HOT SPELLS, BOYS?

MAYOR PORK!

IT WON'T BE LONG BEFORE SEASONALITY RETURNS! MY **STORM PREDICTION CENTER** HAS BEEN ON TOP OF THIS FROM THE START!.... DON'T **YOU** WATCH WEATHER REPORTS, KIDS?

W-W-WEATHER **REPORTS?!** SO... NOT ONLY WERE OUR WISHES **WORTHLESS,** WE SPENT...

...THE **JAMBOREE MONEY** TO FIND OUT! TROOP **A** WILL STAND FOR **"ABASEMENT"** FOREVERMORE!

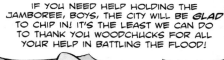

IF YOU NEED HELP HOLDING THE JAMBOREE, BOYS, THE CITY WILL BE **GLAD** TO CHIP IN! IT'S THE LEAST WE CAN DO TO THANK YOU WOODCHUCKS FOR ALL YOUR HELP IN BATTLING THE FLOOD!

AND SO...

THESE TURKEY SANDWICHES ARE **DELICIOUS,** BOYS! HAVE YOU TRIED THEM YET?

NO THANK YOU, SIR! WE DON'T **WISH** TO HAVE ANY TURKEY FOR A GOOD, **LONG** WHILE!

WOODCHUCK JAMBOREE

The End

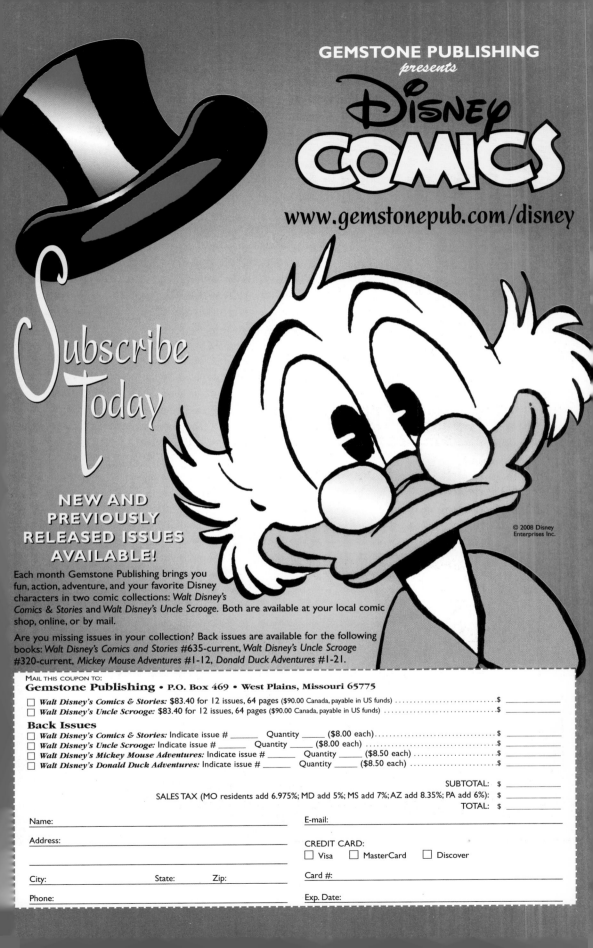

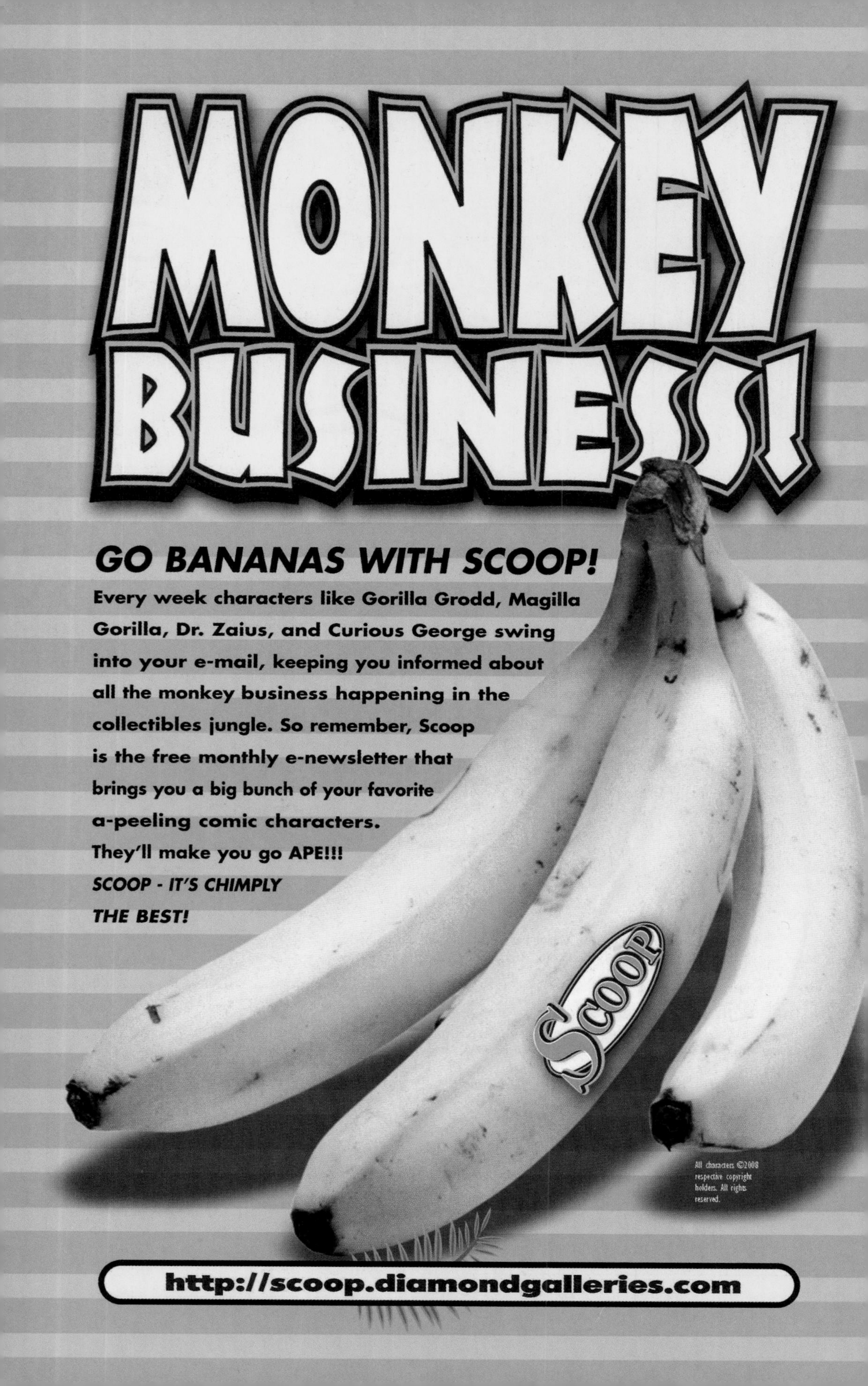
MONKEY BUSINESS!
GO BANANAS WITH SCOOP!
Every week characters like Gorilla Grodd, Magilla Gorilla, Dr. Zaius, and Curious George swing into your e-mail, keeping you informed about all the monkey business happening in the collectibles jungle. So remember, Scoop is the free monthly e-newsletter that brings you a big bunch of your favorite a-peeling comic characters.
They'll make you go APE!!!
SCOOP - IT'S CHIMPLY THE BEST!
Scoop
All characters ©2008 respective copyright holders. All rights reserved.
http://scoop.diamondgalleries.com

Walt Disney's GOOFY in WEATHER OR NOT

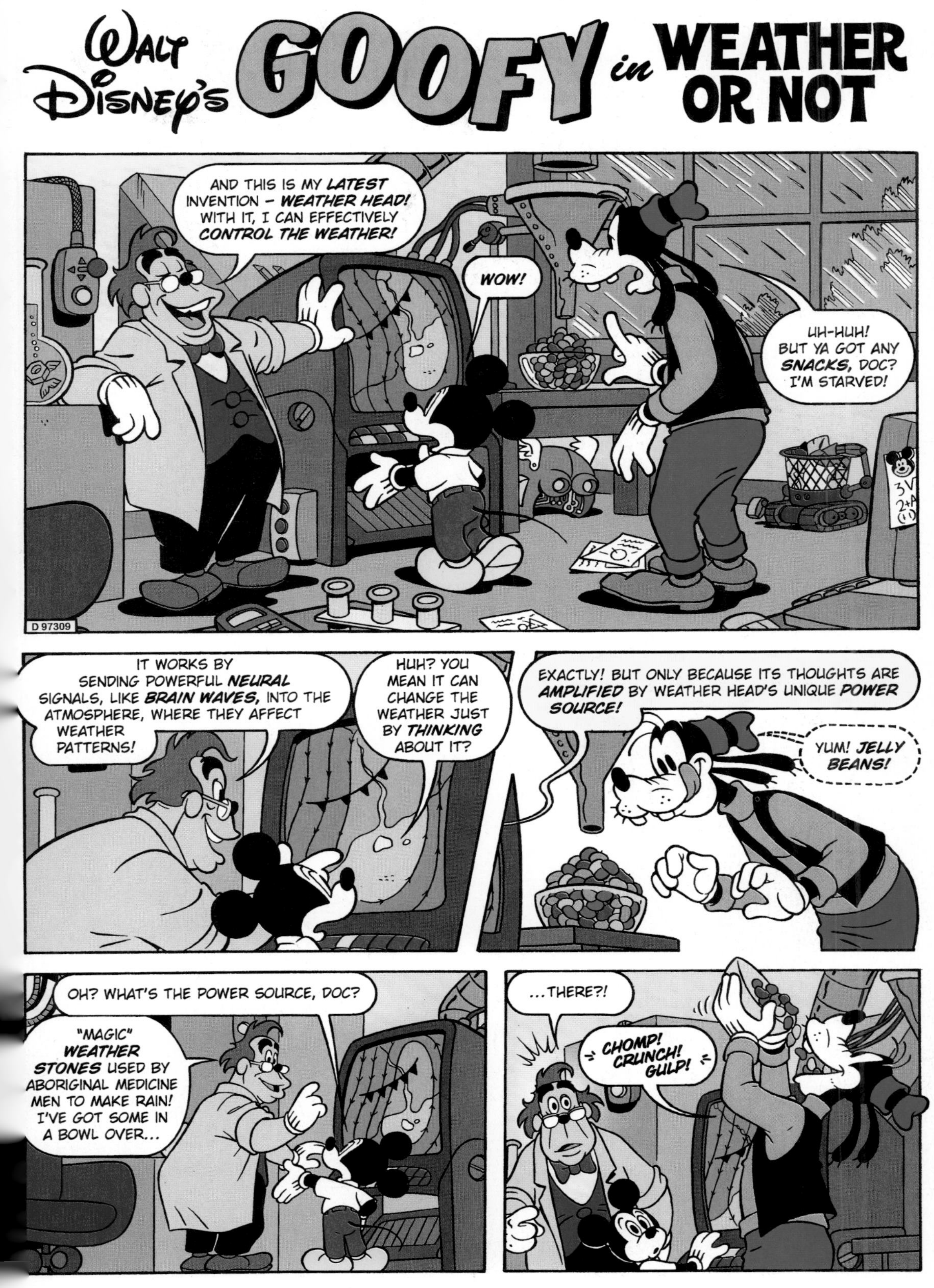
AND THIS IS MY LATEST INVENTION – WEATHER HEAD! WITH IT, I CAN EFFECTIVELY CONTROL THE WEATHER!
WOW!
UH-HUH! BUT YA GOT ANY SNACKS, DOC? I'M STARVED!
D 97309
IT WORKS BY SENDING POWERFUL NEURAL SIGNALS, LIKE BRAIN WAVES, INTO THE ATMOSPHERE, WHERE THEY AFFECT WEATHER PATTERNS!
HUH? YOU MEAN IT CAN CHANGE THE WEATHER JUST BY THINKING ABOUT IT?
EXACTLY! BUT ONLY BECAUSE ITS THOUGHTS ARE AMPLIFIED BY WEATHER HEAD'S UNIQUE POWER SOURCE!
YUM! JELLY BEANS!
OH? WHAT'S THE POWER SOURCE, DOC?
"MAGIC" WEATHER STONES USED BY ABORIGINAL MEDICINE MEN TO MAKE RAIN! I'VE GOT SOME IN A BOWL OVER...
...THERE?!
CHOMP! CRUNCH! GULP!

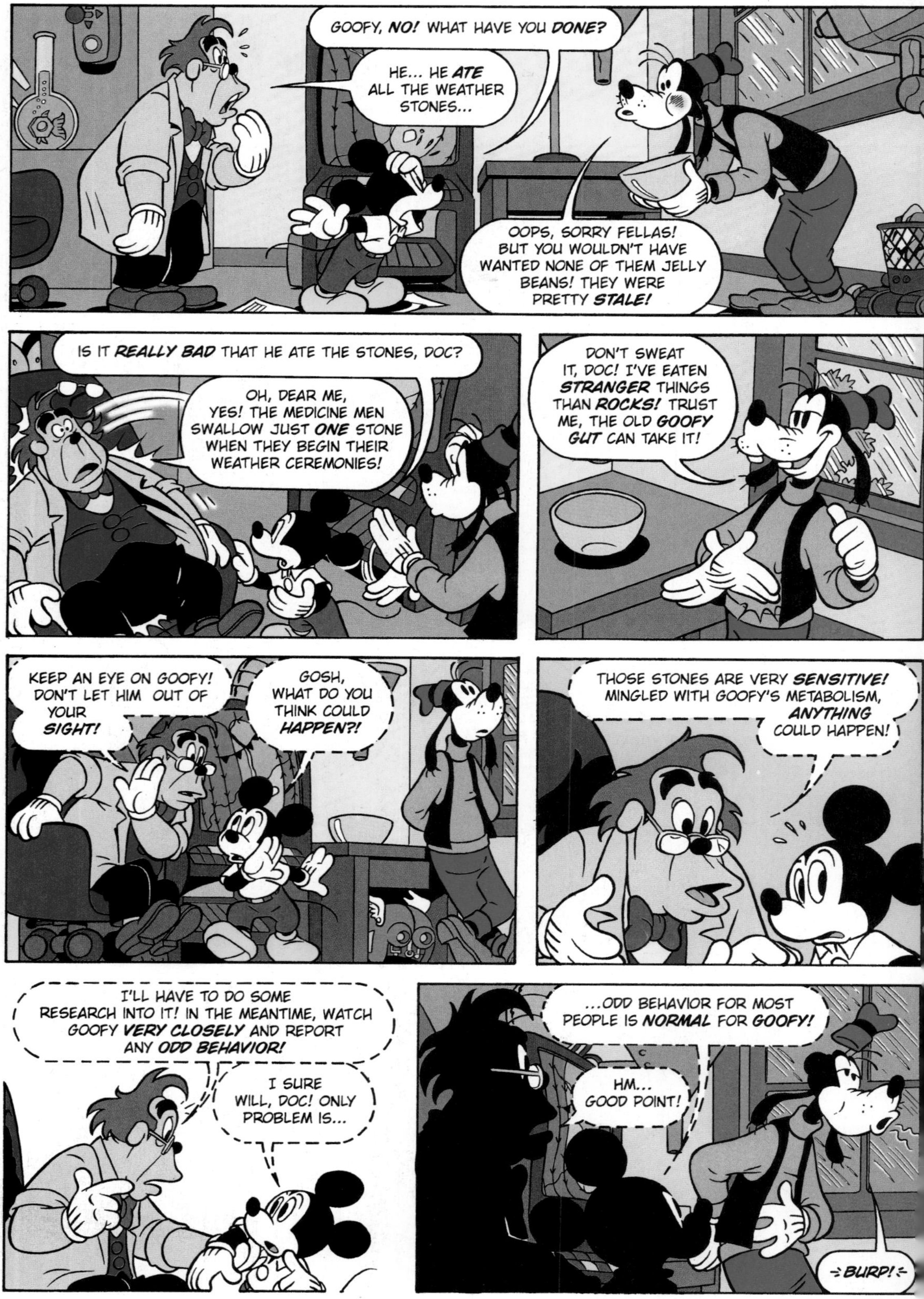
GOOFY, NO! WHAT HAVE YOU DONE?
HE... HE ATE ALL THE WEATHER STONES...
OOPS, SORRY FELLAS! BUT YOU WOULDN'T HAVE WANTED NONE OF THEM JELLY BEANS! THEY WERE PRETTY STALE!
IS IT REALLY BAD THAT HE ATE THE STONES, DOC?
OH, DEAR ME, YES! THE MEDICINE MEN SWALLOW JUST ONE STONE WHEN THEY BEGIN THEIR WEATHER CEREMONIES!
DON'T SWEAT IT, DOC! I'VE EATEN STRANGER THINGS THAN ROCKS! TRUST ME, THE OLD GOOFY GUT CAN TAKE IT!
KEEP AN EYE ON GOOFY! DON'T LET HIM OUT OF YOUR SIGHT!
GOSH, WHAT DO YOU THINK COULD HAPPEN?!
THOSE STONES ARE VERY SENSITIVE! MINGLED WITH GOOFY'S METABOLISM, ANYTHING COULD HAPPEN!
I'LL HAVE TO DO SOME RESEARCH INTO IT! IN THE MEANTIME, WATCH GOOFY VERY CLOSELY AND REPORT ANY ODD BEHAVIOR!
I SURE WILL, DOC! ONLY PROBLEM IS...
...ODD BEHAVIOR FOR MOST PEOPLE IS NORMAL FOR GOOFY!
HM... GOOD POINT!
BURP!

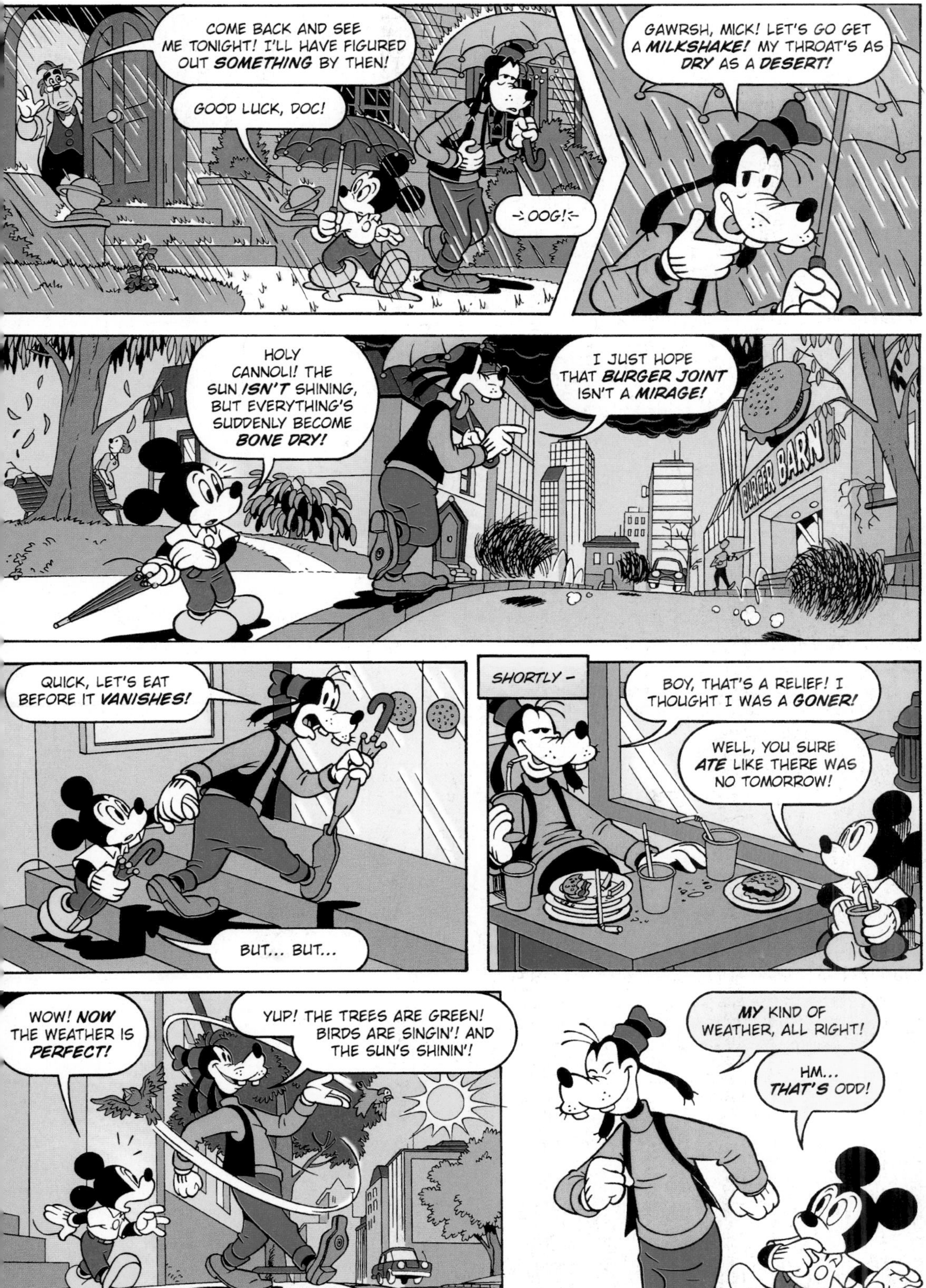
COME BACK AND SEE ME TONIGHT! I'LL HAVE FIGURED OUT SOMETHING BY THEN!
GOOD LUCK, DOC!
-OOG!-
GAWRSH, MICK! LET'S GO GET A MILKSHAKE! MY THROAT'S AS DRY AS A DESERT!
HOLY CANNOLI! THE SUN ISN'T SHINING, BUT EVERYTHING'S SUDDENLY BECOME BONE DRY!
I JUST HOPE THAT BURGER JOINT ISN'T A MIRAGE!
BURGER BARN
QUICK, LET'S EAT BEFORE IT VANISHES!
BUT... BUT...
SHORTLY -
BOY, THAT'S A RELIEF! I THOUGHT I WAS A GONER!
WELL, YOU SURE ATE LIKE THERE WAS NO TOMORROW!
WOW! NOW THE WEATHER IS PERFECT!
YUP! THE TREES ARE GREEN! BIRDS ARE SINGIN'! AND THE SUN'S SHININ'!
MY KIND OF WEATHER, ALL RIGHT!
HM... THAT'S ODD!

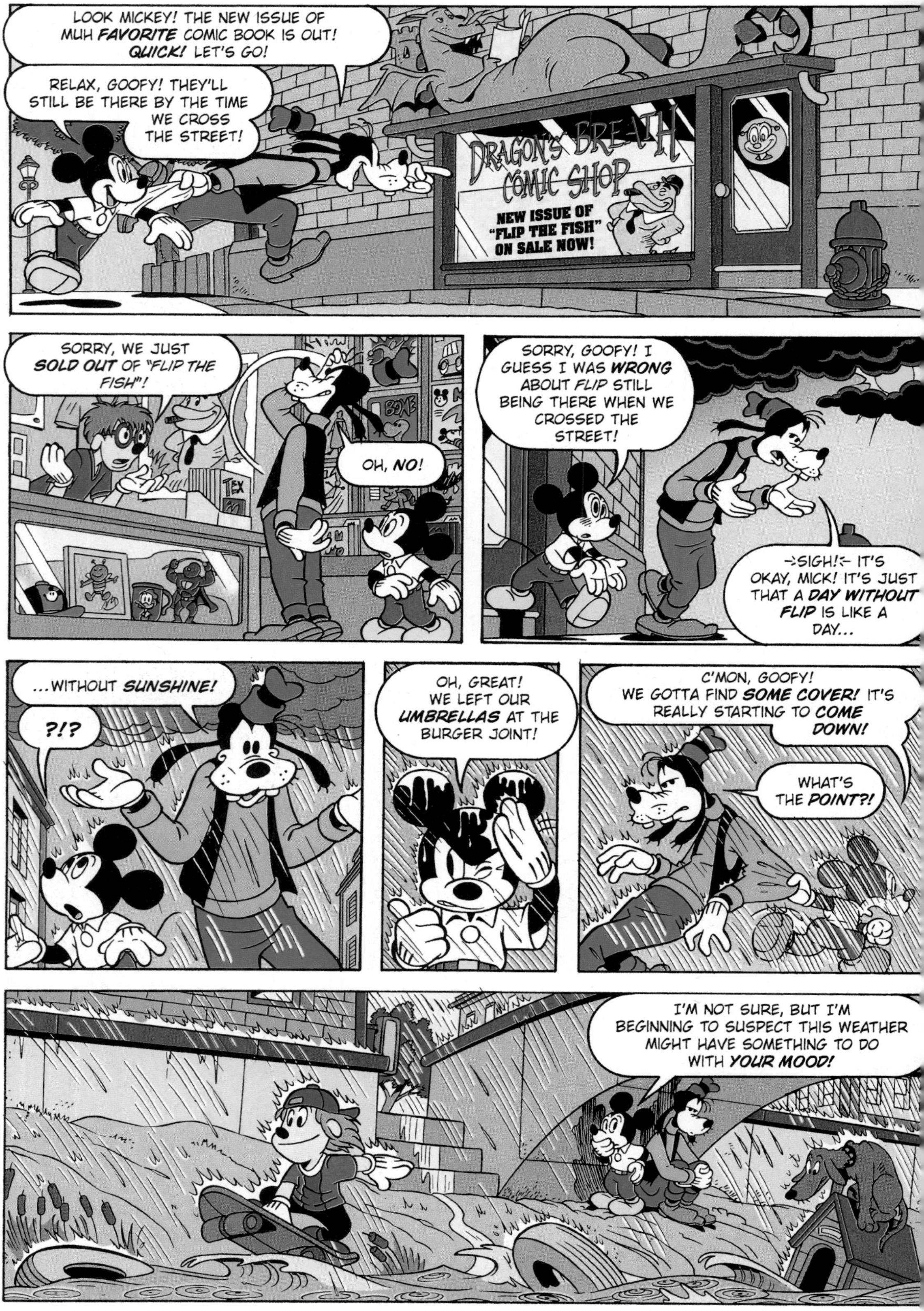

LOOK MICKEY! THE NEW ISSUE OF MUH FAVORITE COMIC BOOK IS OUT! QUICK! LET'S GO!
RELAX, GOOFY! THEY'LL STILL BE THERE BY THE TIME WE CROSS THE STREET!
DRAGON'S BREATH COMIC SHOP
NEW ISSUE OF "FLIP THE FISH" ON SALE NOW!
SORRY, WE JUST SOLD OUT OF "FLIP THE FISH"!
OH, NO!
SORRY, GOOFY! I GUESS I WAS WRONG ABOUT FLIP STILL BEING THERE WHEN WE CROSSED THE STREET!
→SIGH!← IT'S OKAY, MICK! IT'S JUST THAT A DAY WITHOUT FLIP IS LIKE A DAY...
...WITHOUT SUNSHINE!
?!?
OH, GREAT! WE LEFT OUR UMBRELLAS AT THE BURGER JOINT!
C'MON, GOOFY! WE GOTTA FIND SOME COVER! IT'S REALLY STARTING TO COME DOWN!
WHAT'S THE POINT?!
I'M NOT SURE, BUT I'M BEGINNING TO SUSPECT THIS WEATHER MIGHT HAVE SOMETHING TO DO WITH YOUR MOOD!

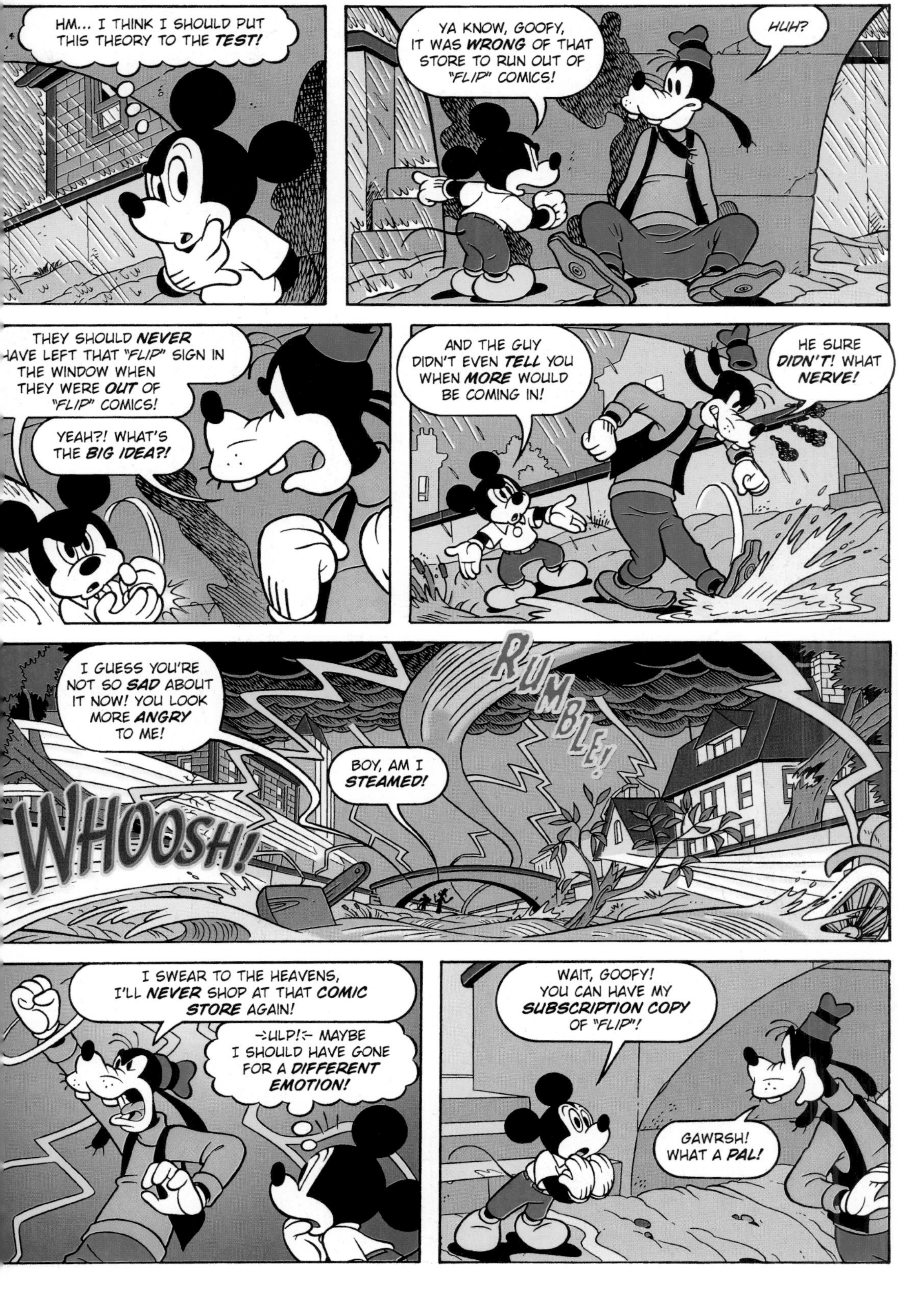
HM... I THINK I SHOULD PUT THIS THEORY TO THE TEST!
YA KNOW, GOOFY, IT WAS WRONG OF THAT STORE TO RUN OUT OF "FLIP" COMICS!
HUH?
THEY SHOULD NEVER HAVE LEFT THAT "FLIP" SIGN IN THE WINDOW WHEN THEY WERE OUT OF "FLIP" COMICS!
YEAH?! WHAT'S THE BIG IDEA?!
AND THE GUY DIDN'T EVEN TELL YOU WHEN MORE WOULD BE COMING IN!
HE SURE DIDN'T! WHAT NERVE!
I GUESS YOU'RE NOT SO SAD ABOUT IT NOW! YOU LOOK MORE ANGRY TO ME!
RUMBLE!
BOY, AM I STEAMED!
WHOOSH!
I SWEAR TO THE HEAVENS, I'LL NEVER SHOP AT THAT COMIC STORE AGAIN!
-ULP!- MAYBE I SHOULD HAVE GONE FOR A DIFFERENT EMOTION!
WAIT, GOOFY! YOU CAN HAVE MY SUBSCRIPTION COPY OF "FLIP"!
GAWRSH! WHAT A PAL!

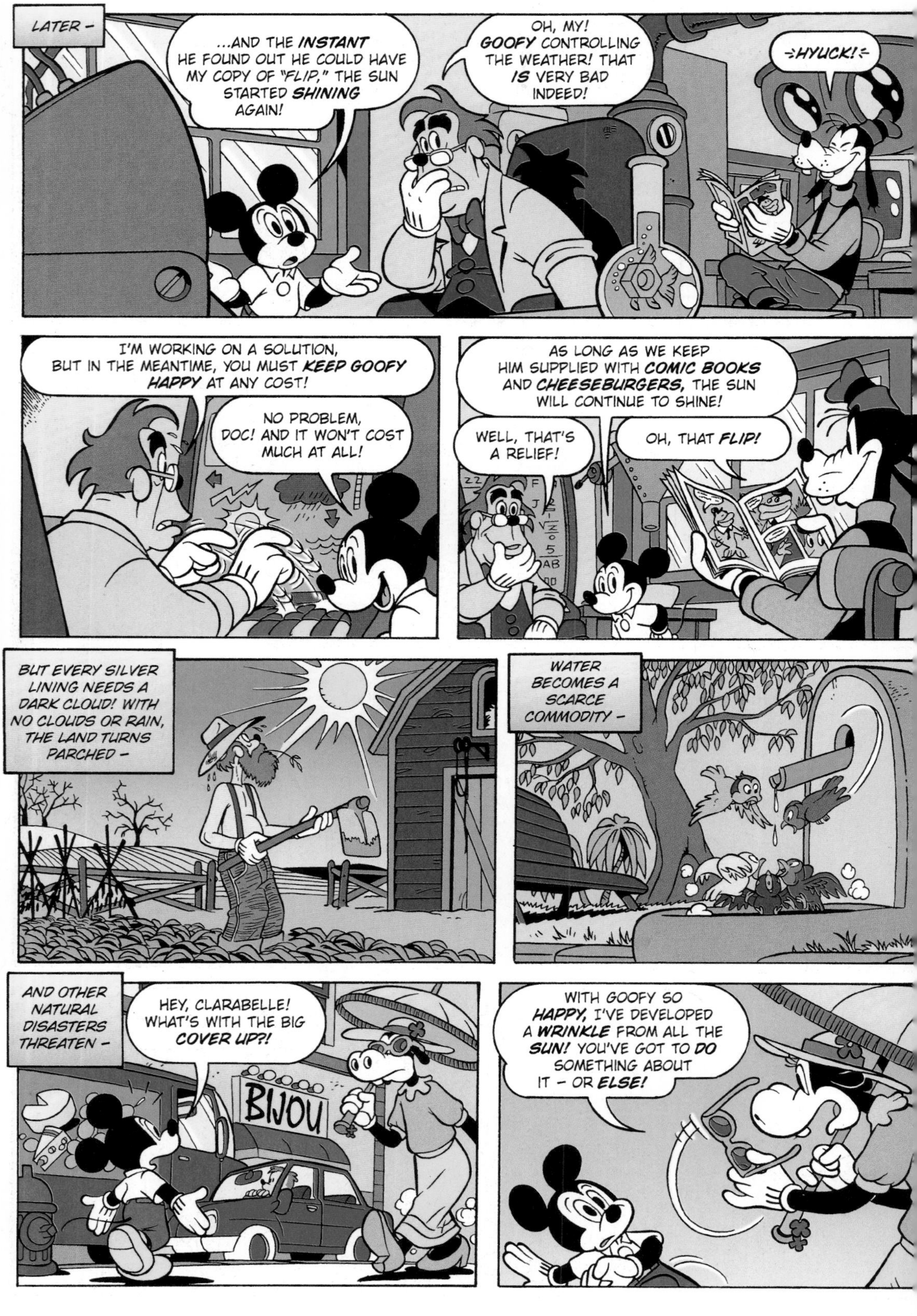
LATER –
...AND THE INSTANT HE FOUND OUT HE COULD HAVE MY COPY OF "FLIP," THE SUN STARTED SHINING AGAIN!
OH, MY! GOOFY CONTROLLING THE WEATHER! THAT IS VERY BAD INDEED!
-HYUCK!-
I'M WORKING ON A SOLUTION, BUT IN THE MEANTIME, YOU MUST KEEP GOOFY HAPPY AT ANY COST!
NO PROBLEM, DOC! AND IT WON'T COST MUCH AT ALL!
AS LONG AS WE KEEP HIM SUPPLIED WITH COMIC BOOKS AND CHEESEBURGERS, THE SUN WILL CONTINUE TO SHINE!
WELL, THAT'S A RELIEF!
OH, THAT FLIP!
BUT EVERY SILVER LINING NEEDS A DARK CLOUD! WITH NO CLOUDS OR RAIN, THE LAND TURNS PARCHED –
WATER BECOMES A SCARCE COMMODITY –
AND OTHER NATURAL DISASTERS THREATEN –
HEY, CLARABELLE! WHAT'S WITH THE BIG COVER UP?!
BIJOU
WITH GOOFY SO HAPPY, I'VE DEVELOPED A WRINKLE FROM ALL THE SUN! YOU'VE GOT TO DO SOMETHING ABOUT IT – OR ELSE!

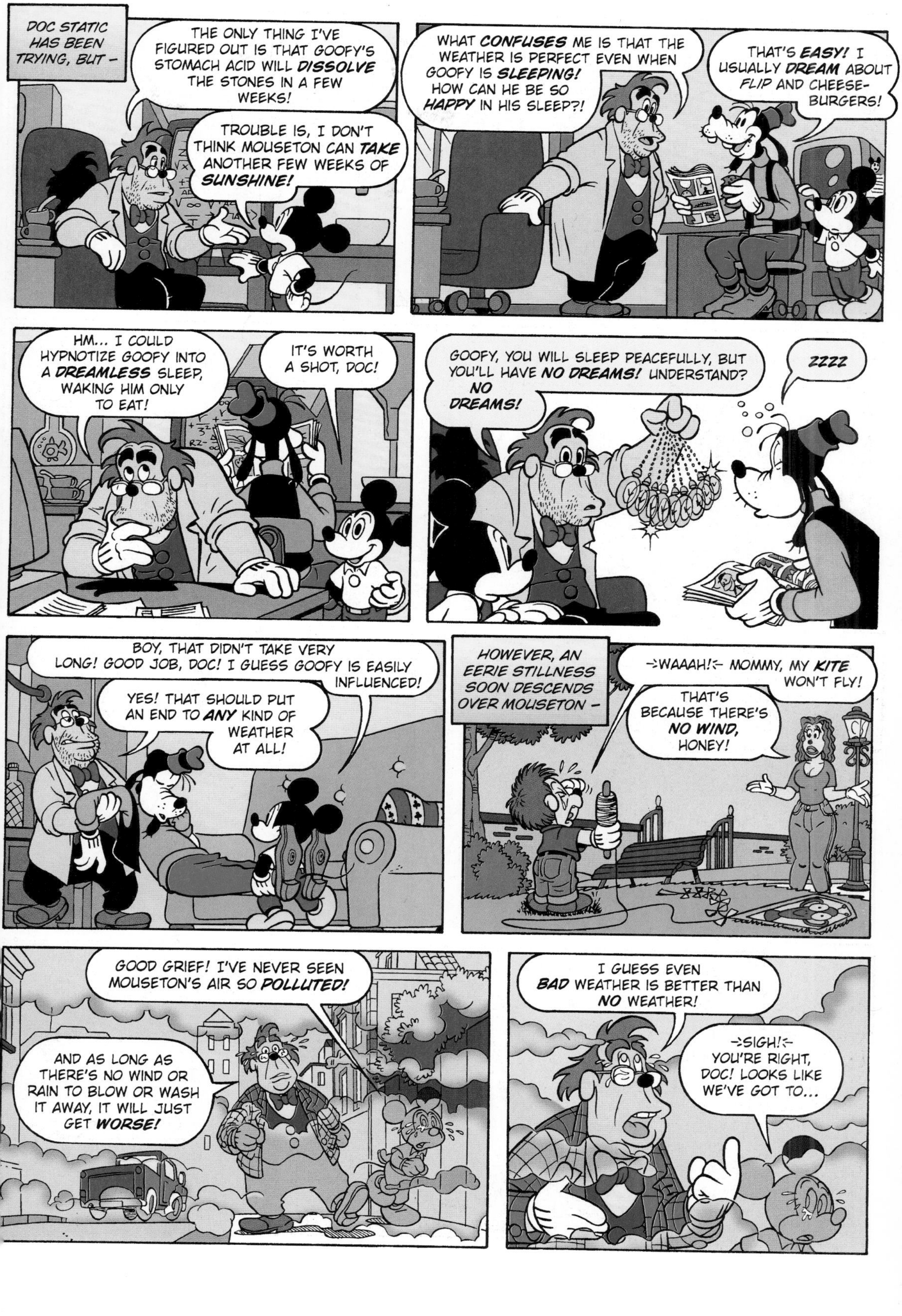
DOC STATIC HAS BEEN TRYING, BUT –
THE ONLY THING I'VE FIGURED OUT IS THAT GOOFY'S STOMACH ACID WILL DISSOLVE THE STONES IN A FEW WEEKS!
TROUBLE IS, I DON'T THINK MOUSETON CAN TAKE ANOTHER FEW WEEKS OF SUNSHINE!
WHAT CONFUSES ME IS THAT THE WEATHER IS PERFECT EVEN WHEN GOOFY IS SLEEPING! HOW CAN HE BE SO HAPPY IN HIS SLEEP?!
THAT'S EASY! I USUALLY DREAM ABOUT FLIP AND CHEESE-BURGERS!
HM... I COULD HYPNOTIZE GOOFY INTO A DREAMLESS SLEEP, WAKING HIM ONLY TO EAT!
IT'S WORTH A SHOT, DOC!
GOOFY, YOU WILL SLEEP PEACEFULLY, BUT YOU'LL HAVE NO DREAMS! UNDERSTAND? NO DREAMS!
ZZZZ
BOY, THAT DIDN'T TAKE VERY LONG! GOOD JOB, DOC! I GUESS GOOFY IS EASILY INFLUENCED!
YES! THAT SHOULD PUT AN END TO ANY KIND OF WEATHER AT ALL!
HOWEVER, AN EERIE STILLNESS SOON DESCENDS OVER MOUSETON –
-WAAAH!- MOMMY, MY KITE WON'T FLY!
THAT'S BECAUSE THERE'S NO WIND, HONEY!
GOOD GRIEF! I'VE NEVER SEEN MOUSETON'S AIR SO POLLUTED!
AND AS LONG AS THERE'S NO WIND OR RAIN TO BLOW OR WASH IT AWAY, IT WILL JUST GET WORSE!
I GUESS EVEN BAD WEATHER IS BETTER THAN NO WEATHER!
-SIGH!- YOU'RE RIGHT, DOC! LOOKS LIKE WE'VE GOT TO...

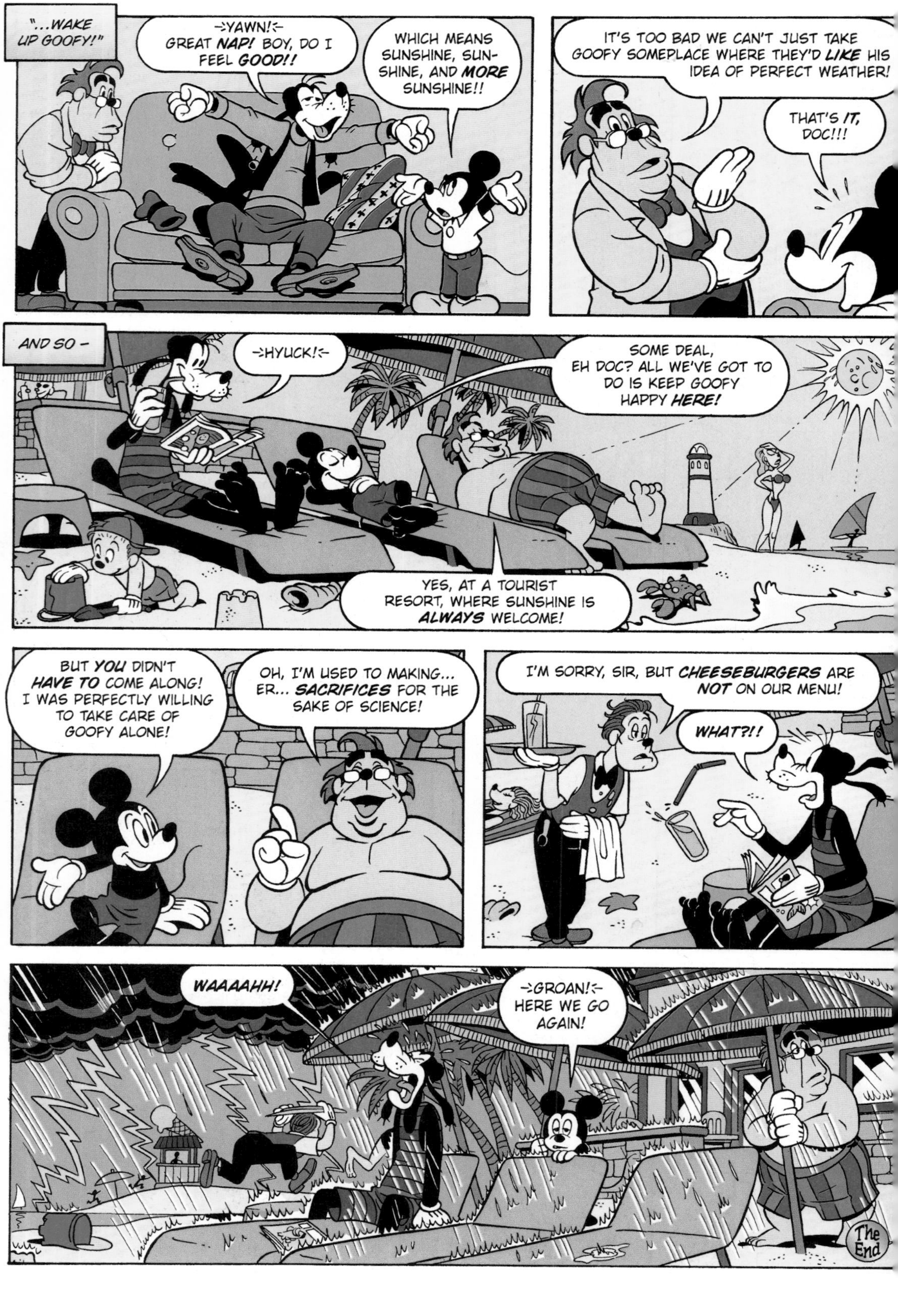
"...WAKE UP GOOFY!"
-YAWN!- GREAT NAP! BOY, DO I FEEL GOOD!!
WHICH MEANS SUNSHINE, SUNSHINE, AND MORE SUNSHINE!!
IT'S TOO BAD WE CAN'T JUST TAKE GOOFY SOMEPLACE WHERE THEY'D LIKE HIS IDEA OF PERFECT WEATHER!
THAT'S IT, DOC!!!
AND SO -
-HYUCK!-
SOME DEAL, EH DOC? ALL WE'VE GOT TO DO IS KEEP GOOFY HAPPY HERE!
YES, AT A TOURIST RESORT, WHERE SUNSHINE IS ALWAYS WELCOME!
BUT YOU DIDN'T HAVE TO COME ALONG! I WAS PERFECTLY WILLING TO TAKE CARE OF GOOFY ALONE!
OH, I'M USED TO MAKING... ER... SACRIFICES FOR THE SAKE OF SCIENCE!
I'M SORRY, SIR, BUT CHEESEBURGERS ARE NOT ON OUR MENU!
WHAT?!!
WAAAAHH!
-GROAN!- HERE WE GO AGAIN!
The End

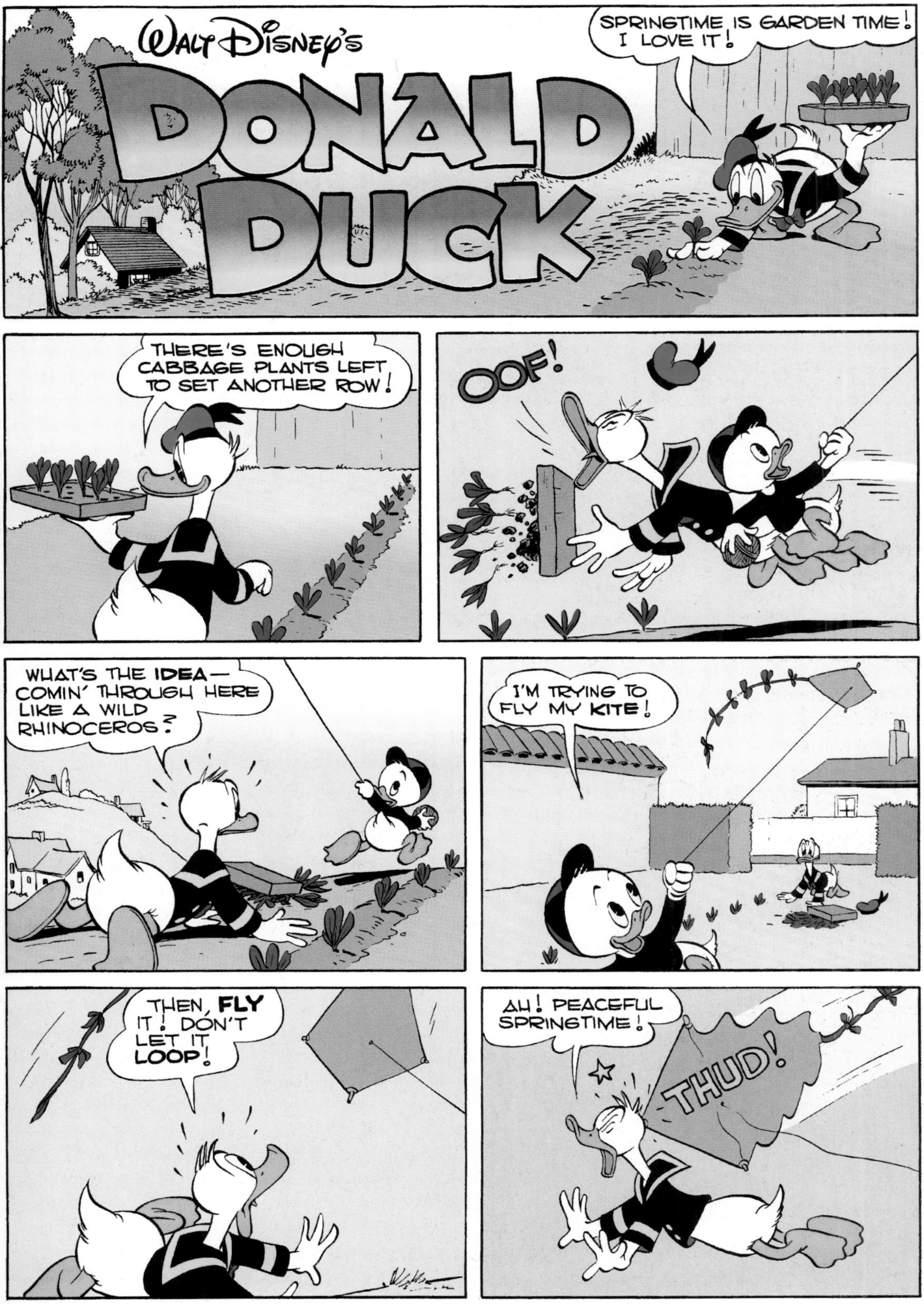
WALT DISNEY'S
DONALD DUCK
SPRINGTIME IS GARDEN TIME! I LOVE IT!
THERE'S ENOUGH CABBAGE PLANTS LEFT TO SET ANOTHER ROW!
OOF!
WHAT'S THE IDEA— COMIN' THROUGH HERE LIKE A WILD RHINOCEROS?
I'M TRYING TO FLY MY KITE!
THEN, FLY IT! DON'T LET IT LOOP!
AH! PEACEFUL SPRINGTIME!
THUD!

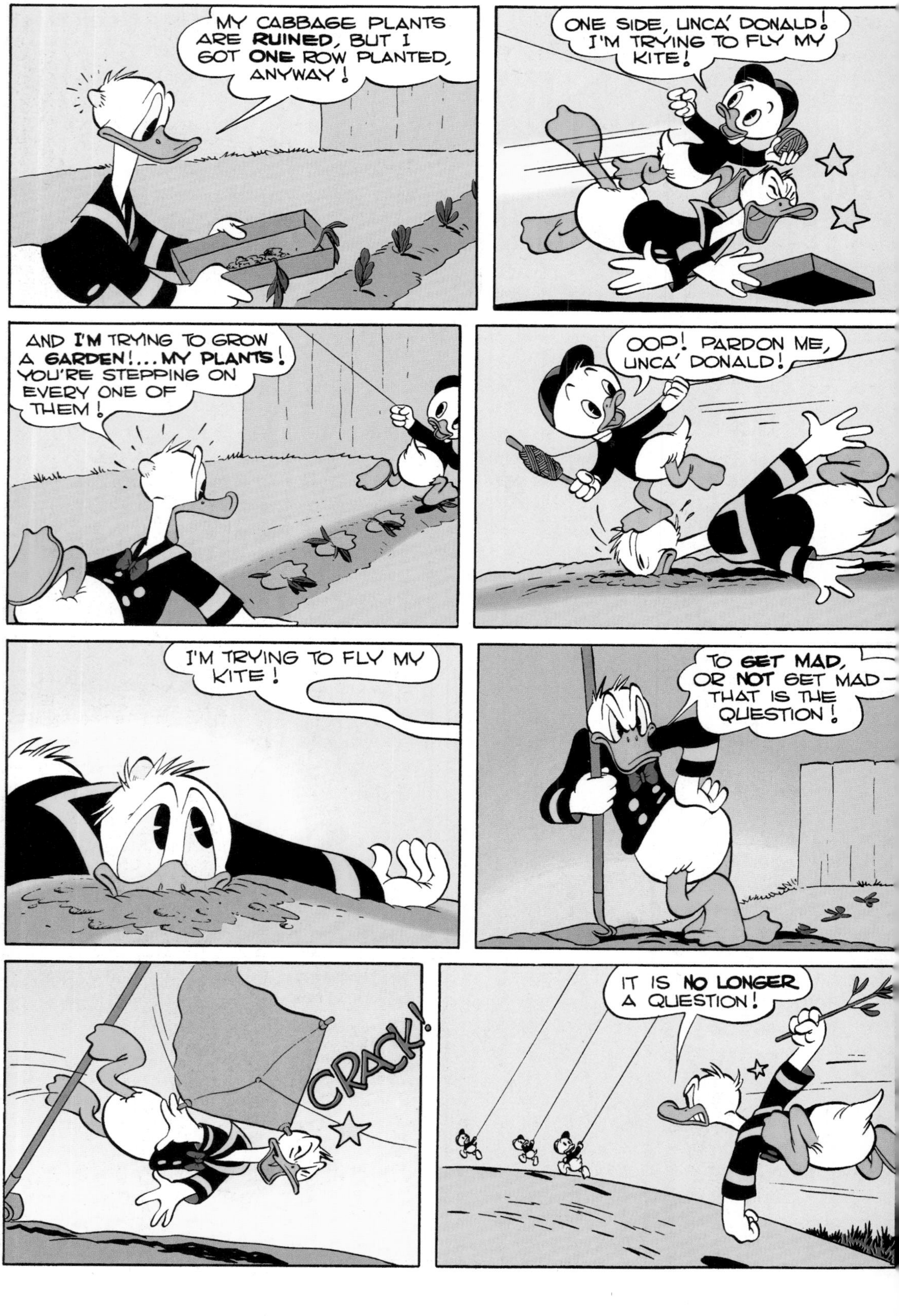
MY CABBAGE PLANTS ARE RUINED, BUT I GOT ONE ROW PLANTED, ANYWAY!
ONE SIDE, UNCA' DONALD! I'M TRYING TO FLY MY KITE!
AND I'M TRYING TO GROW A GARDEN!... MY PLANTS! YOU'RE STEPPING ON EVERY ONE OF THEM!
OOP! PARDON ME, UNCA' DONALD!
I'M TRYING TO FLY MY KITE!
TO GET MAD, OR NOT GET MAD- THAT IS THE QUESTION!
CRACK!
IT IS NO LONGER A QUESTION!

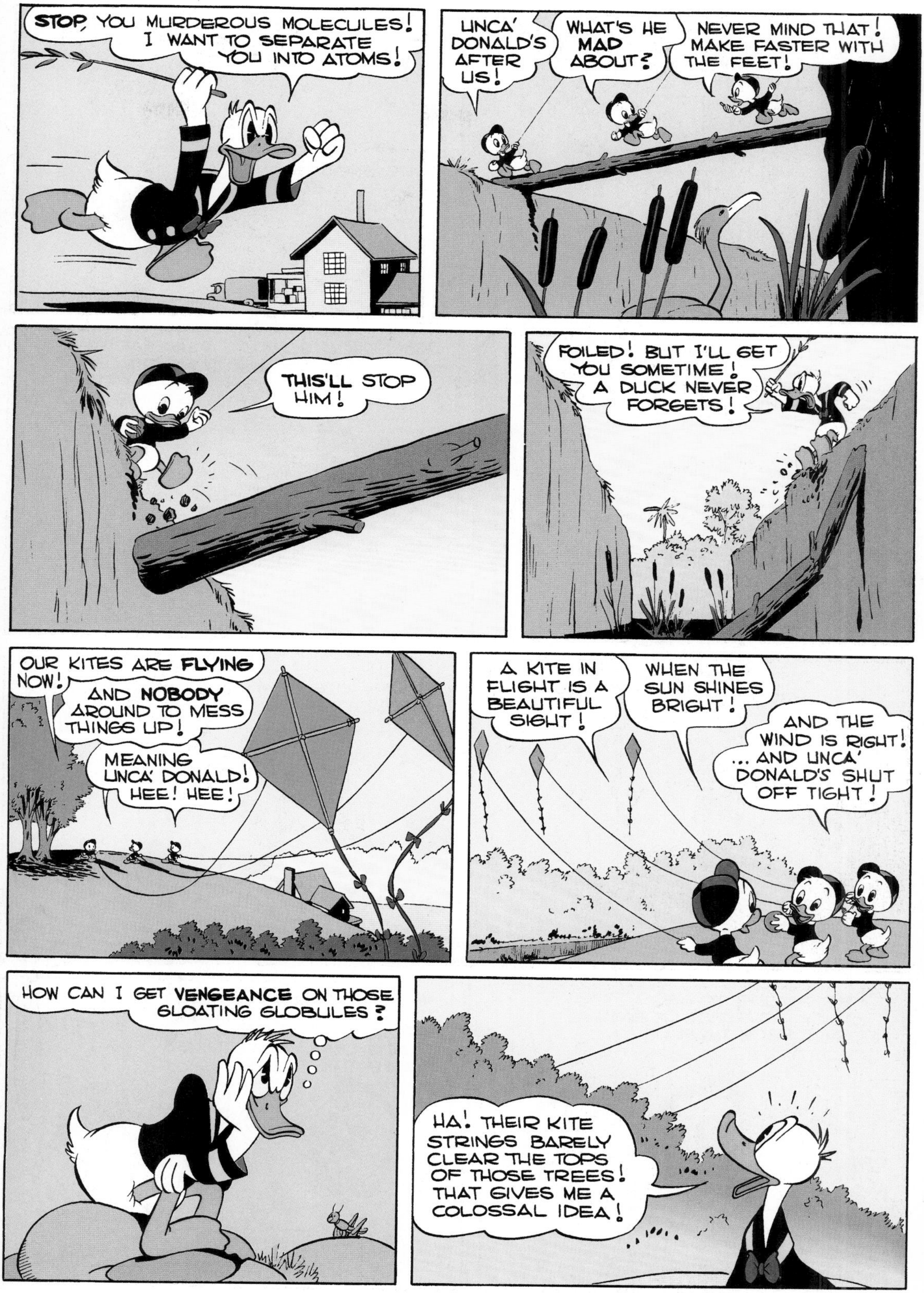
STOP, YOU MURDEROUS MOLECULES! I WANT TO SEPARATE YOU INTO ATOMS!
UNCA' DONALD'S AFTER US!
WHAT'S HE MAD ABOUT?
NEVER MIND THAT! MAKE FASTER WITH THE FEET!
THIS'LL STOP HIM!
FOILED! BUT I'LL GET YOU SOMETIME! A DUCK NEVER FORGETS!
OUR KITES ARE FLYING NOW!
AND NOBODY AROUND TO MESS THINGS UP!
MEANING UNCA' DONALD! HEE! HEE!
A KITE IN FLIGHT IS A BEAUTIFUL SIGHT!
WHEN THE SUN SHINES BRIGHT!
AND THE WIND IS RIGHT!
... AND UNCA' DONALD'S SHUT OFF TIGHT!
HOW CAN I GET VENGEANCE ON THOSE GLOATING GLOBULES?
HA! THEIR KITE STRINGS BARELY CLEAR THE TOPS OF THOSE TREES! THAT GIVES ME A COLOSSAL IDEA!

LATER! THIS IS A LOT OF WORK, BUT THE FUN WILL BE WORTH IT!

REVENGE IS SWEET, BUT **TRIPLE** VENGEANCE IS CARAMEL SUNDAE!

I'LL LIGHT THIS **ROCKET!** THE ROCKET WILL FOLLOW THE **STRING!** THE STRING LEADS TO THE **KITE!** NEED I SAY **MORE?**

HEY! UNCA' DONALD IS UP TO SOMETHING!

HE HAS TIED A **ROCKET** TO YOUR KITE STRING!

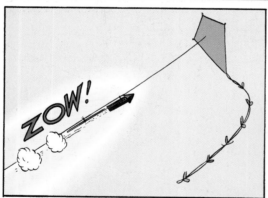

ZOW!

HEH! HEH! HEH! **ONE** KITE DOWN! TWO TO GO!

BOOM!

MOVE YOUR KITES! QUICK! OR UNCA' DONALD WILL BLOW **THEM** UP, TOO!

WE **CAN'T MOVE** FROM HERE! THIS HIGH GROUND IS THE ONLY PLACE OUR KITE STRINGS CLEAR THE TREES!

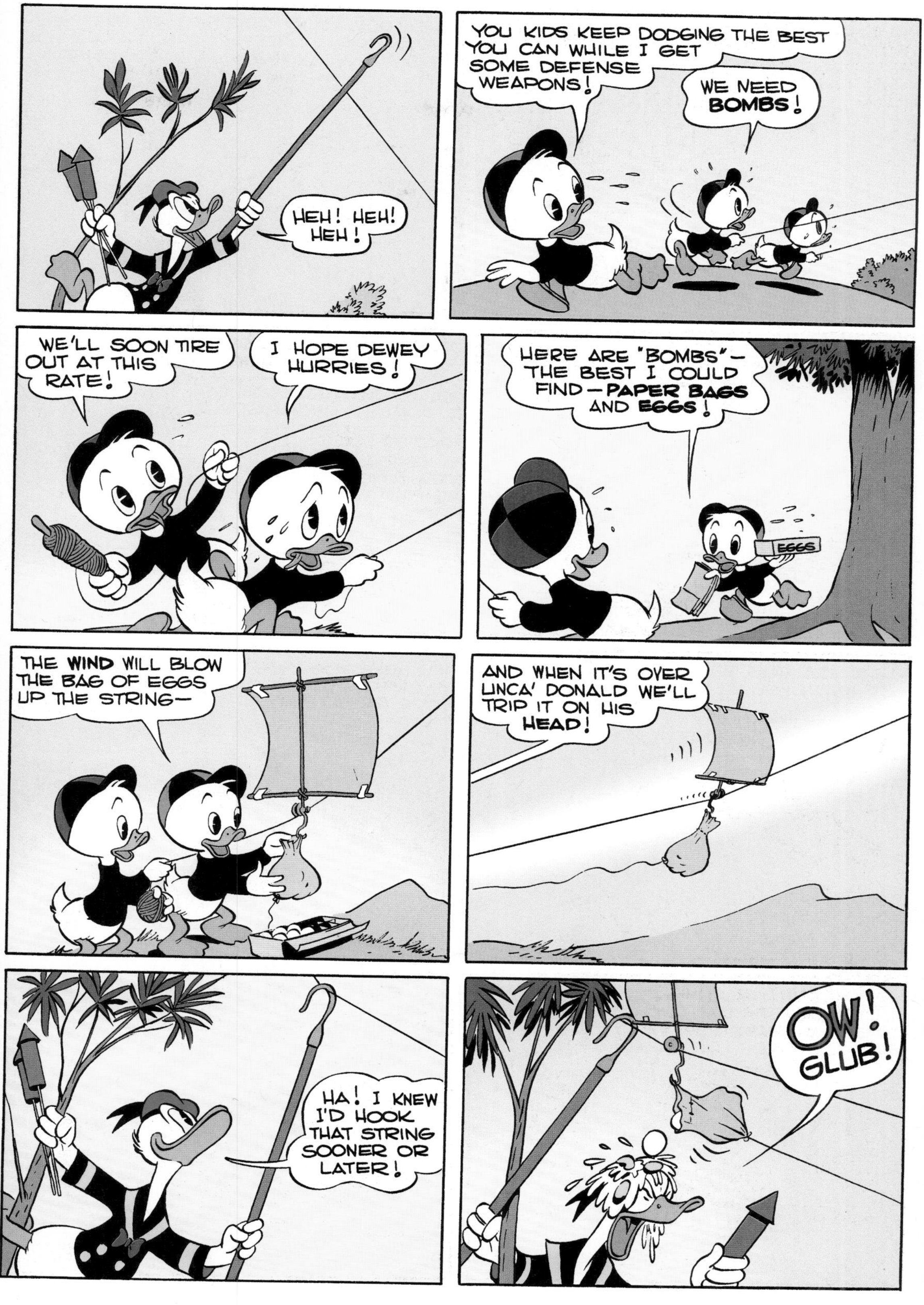
HEH! HEH! HEH!
YOU KIDS KEEP DODGING THE BEST YOU CAN WHILE I GET SOME DEFENSE WEAPONS!
WE NEED BOMBS!
WE'LL SOON TIRE OUT AT THIS RATE!
I HOPE DEWEY HURRIES!
HERE ARE "BOMBS"— THE BEST I COULD FIND—PAPER BAGS AND EGGS!
EGGS
THE WIND WILL BLOW THE BAG OF EGGS UP THE STRING—
AND WHEN IT'S OVER UNCA' DONALD WE'LL TRIP IT ON HIS HEAD!
HA! I KNEW I'D HOOK THAT STRING SOONER OR LATER!
OW! GLUB!

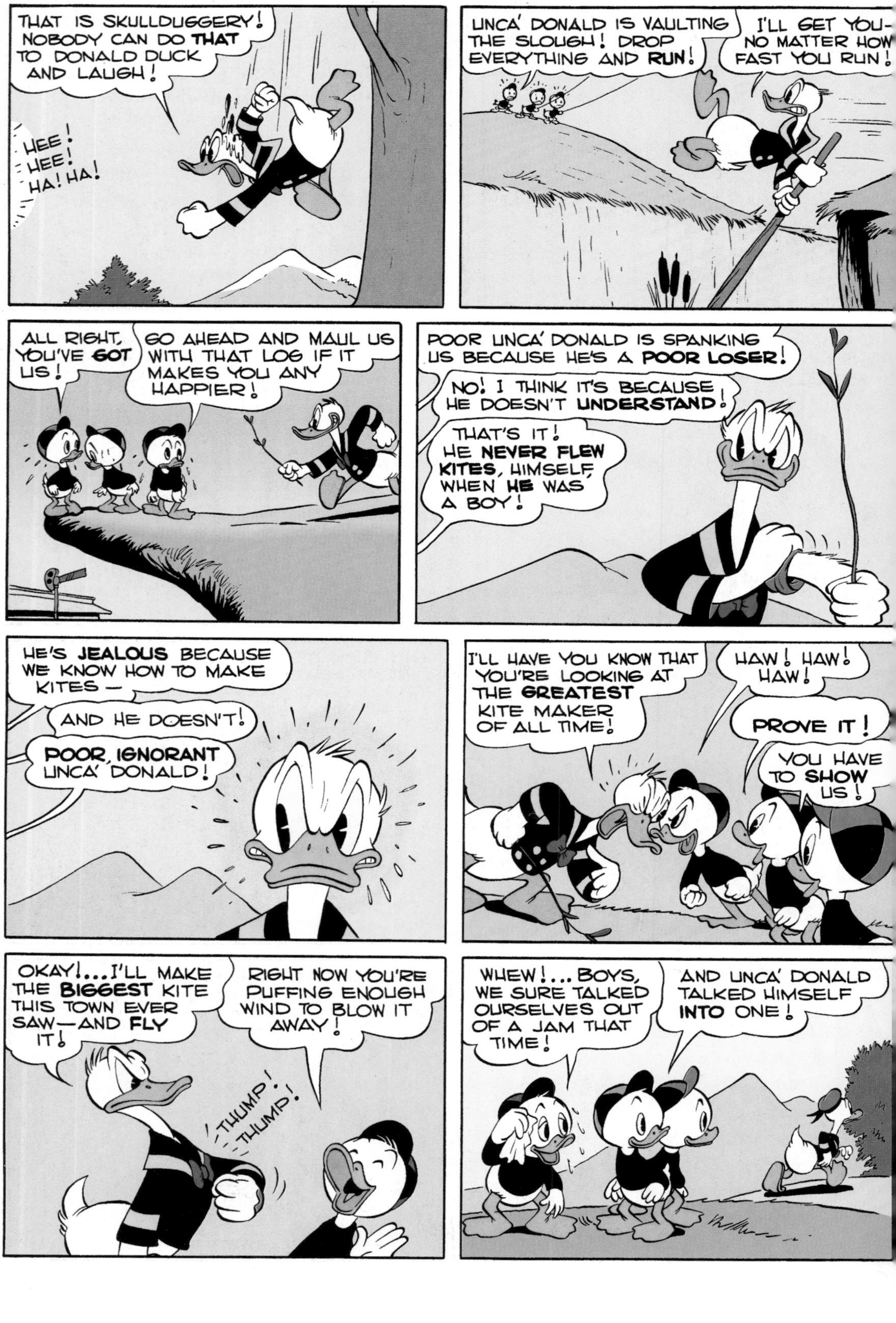
THAT IS SKULLDUGGERY! NOBODY CAN DO THAT TO DONALD DUCK AND LAUGH!
HEE! HEE! HA! HA!
UNCA' DONALD IS VAULTING THE SLOUGH! DROP EVERYTHING AND RUN!
I'LL GET YOU— NO MATTER HOW FAST YOU RUN!
ALL RIGHT, YOU'VE GOT US!
GO AHEAD AND MAUL US WITH THAT LOG IF IT MAKES YOU ANY HAPPIER!
POOR UNCA' DONALD IS SPANKING US BECAUSE HE'S A POOR LOSER!
NO! I THINK IT'S BECAUSE HE DOESN'T UNDERSTAND!
THAT'S IT! HE NEVER FLEW KITES, HIMSELF, WHEN HE WAS A BOY!
HE'S JEALOUS BECAUSE WE KNOW HOW TO MAKE KITES —
AND HE DOESN'T!
POOR, IGNORANT UNCA' DONALD!
I'LL HAVE YOU KNOW THAT YOU'RE LOOKING AT THE GREATEST KITE MAKER OF ALL TIME!
HAW! HAW! HAW!
PROVE IT!
YOU HAVE TO SHOW US!
OKAY!...I'LL MAKE THE BIGGEST KITE THIS TOWN EVER SAW—AND FLY IT!
RIGHT NOW YOU'RE PUFFING ENOUGH WIND TO BLOW IT AWAY!
THUMP! THUMP!
WHEW!... BOYS, WE SURE TALKED OURSELVES OUT OF A JAM THAT TIME!
AND UNCA' DONALD TALKED HIMSELF INTO ONE!

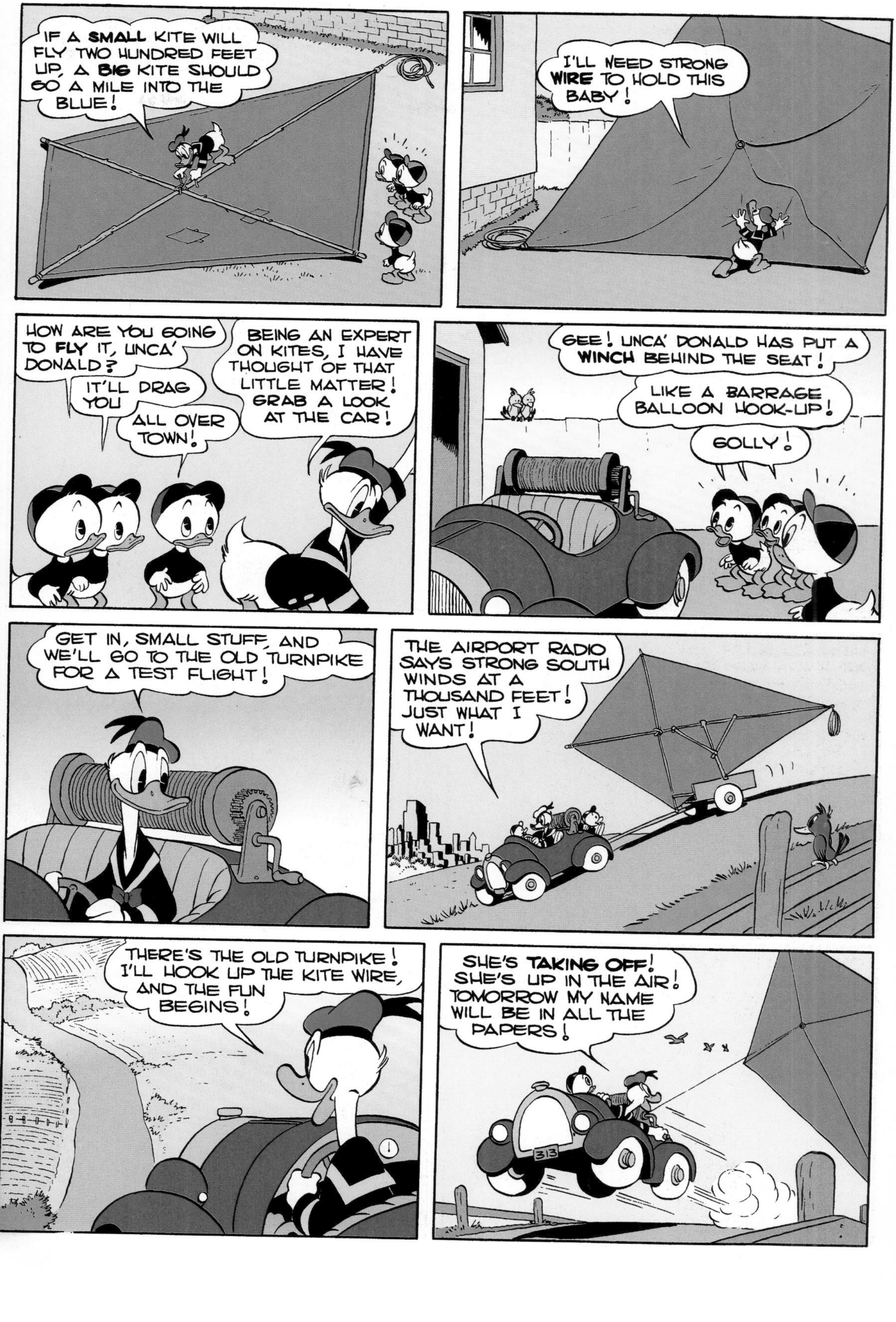
IF A **SMALL** KITE WILL FLY TWO HUNDRED FEET UP, A **BIG** KITE SHOULD GO A MILE INTO THE BLUE!
I'LL NEED STRONG **WIRE** TO HOLD THIS BABY!
HOW ARE YOU GOING TO **FLY** IT, UNCA' DONALD?
IT'LL DRAG YOU
ALL OVER TOWN!
BEING AN EXPERT ON KITES, I HAVE THOUGHT OF THAT LITTLE MATTER! GRAB A LOOK AT THE CAR!
GEE! UNCA' DONALD HAS PUT A **WINCH** BEHIND THE SEAT!
LIKE A BARRAGE BALLOON HOOK-UP!
GOLLY!
GET IN, SMALL STUFF, AND WE'LL GO TO THE OLD TURNPIKE FOR A TEST FLIGHT!
THE AIRPORT RADIO SAYS STRONG SOUTH WINDS AT A THOUSAND FEET! JUST WHAT I WANT!
THERE'S THE OLD TURNPIKE! I'LL HOOK UP THE KITE WIRE, AND THE FUN BEGINS!
SHE'S **TAKING OFF**! SHE'S UP IN THE AIR! TOMORROW MY NAME WILL BE IN ALL THE PAPERS!
313

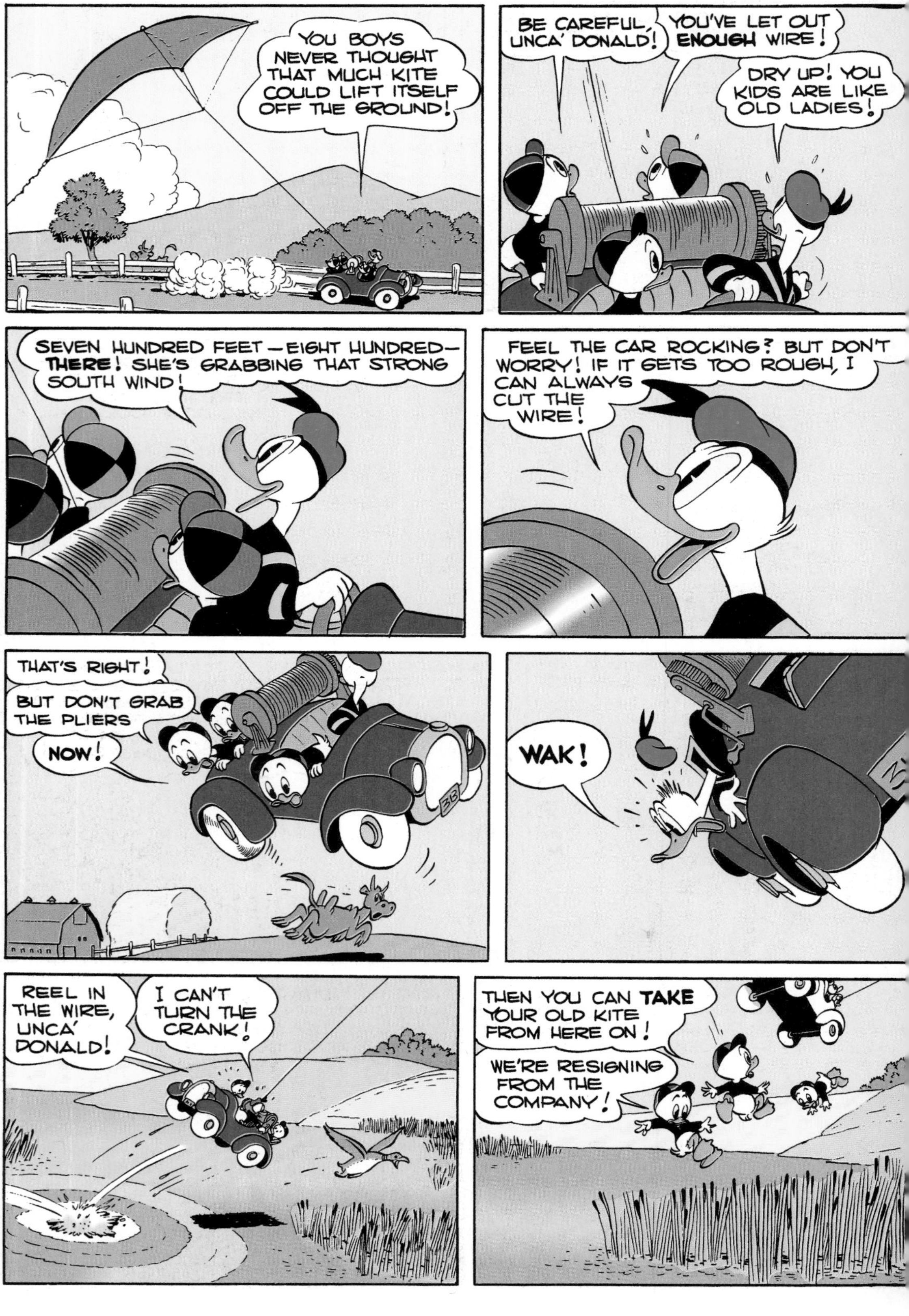
YOU BOYS NEVER THOUGHT THAT MUCH KITE COULD LIFT ITSELF OFF THE GROUND!
BE CAREFUL, UNCA' DONALD!
YOU'VE LET OUT ENOUGH WIRE!
DRY UP! YOU KIDS ARE LIKE OLD LADIES!
SEVEN HUNDRED FEET—EIGHT HUNDRED—THERE! SHE'S GRABBING THAT STRONG SOUTH WIND!
FEEL THE CAR ROCKING? BUT DON'T WORRY! IF IT GETS TOO ROUGH, I CAN ALWAYS CUT THE WIRE!
THAT'S RIGHT!
BUT DON'T GRAB THE PLIERS
NOW!
WAK!
REEL IN THE WIRE, UNCA' DONALD!
I CAN'T TURN THE CRANK!
THEN YOU CAN TAKE YOUR OLD KITE FROM HERE ON!
WE'RE RESIGNING FROM THE COMPANY!

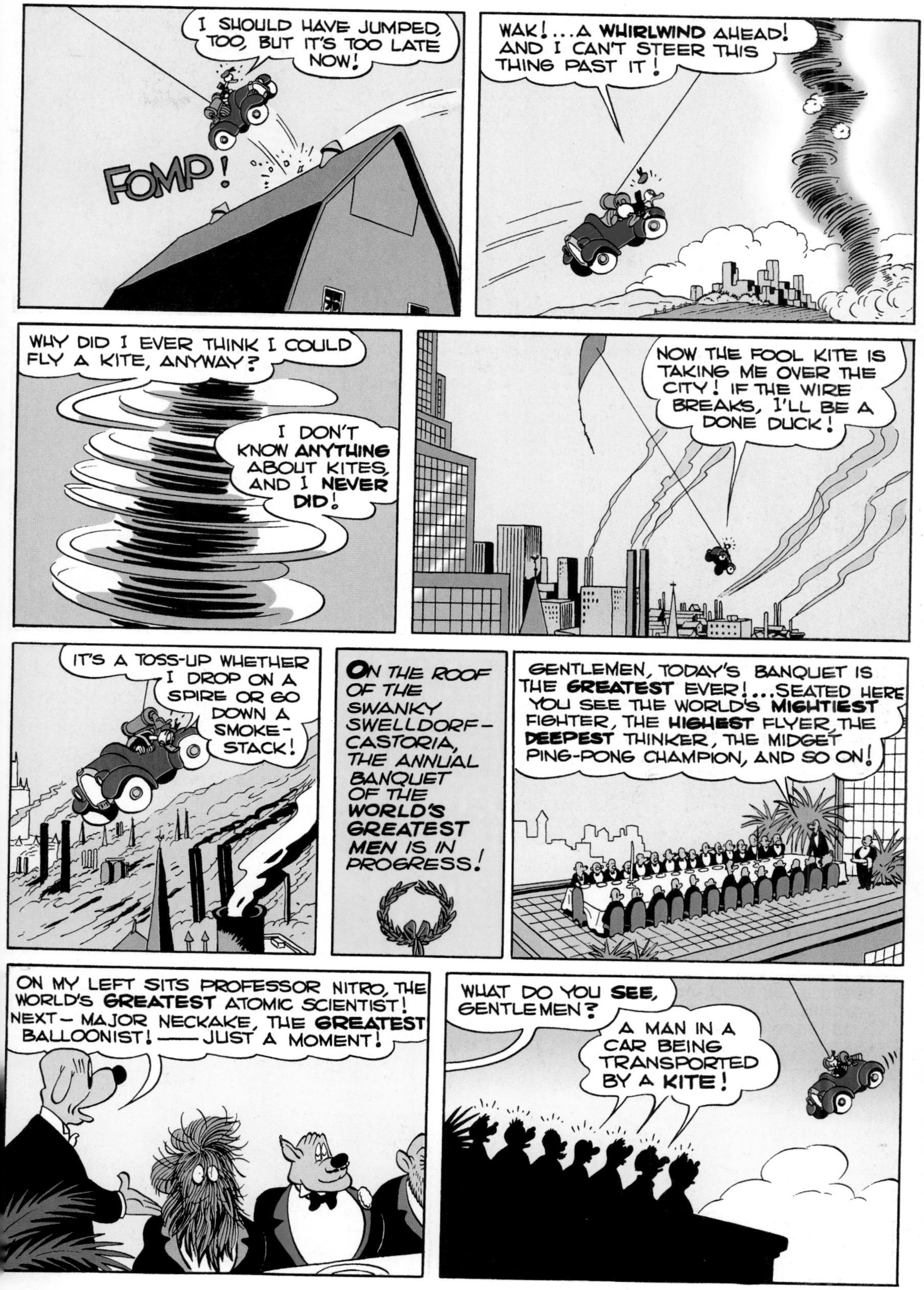
I SHOULD HAVE JUMPED, TOO, BUT IT'S TOO LATE NOW!
FOMP!
WAK!...A WHIRLWIND AHEAD! AND I CAN'T STEER THIS THING PAST IT!
WHY DID I EVER THINK I COULD FLY A KITE, ANYWAY?
I DON'T KNOW ANYTHING ABOUT KITES, AND I NEVER DID!
NOW THE FOOL KITE IS TAKING ME OVER THE CITY! IF THE WIRE BREAKS, I'LL BE A DONE DUCK!
IT'S A TOSS-UP WHETHER I DROP ON A SPIRE OR GO DOWN A SMOKE-STACK!
ON THE ROOF OF THE SWANKY SWELLDORF-CASTORIA, THE ANNUAL BANQUET OF THE WORLD'S GREATEST MEN IS IN PROGRESS!
GENTLEMEN, TODAY'S BANQUET IS THE GREATEST EVER!...SEATED HERE YOU SEE THE WORLD'S MIGHTIEST FIGHTER, THE HIGHEST FLYER, THE DEEPEST THINKER, THE MIDGET PING-PONG CHAMPION, AND SO ON!
ON MY LEFT SITS PROFESSOR NITRO, THE WORLD'S GREATEST ATOMIC SCIENTIST! NEXT— MAJOR NECKAKE, THE GREATEST BALLOONIST! —— JUST A MOMENT!
WHAT DO YOU SEE, GENTLEMEN?
A MAN IN A CAR BEING TRANSPORTED BY A KITE!

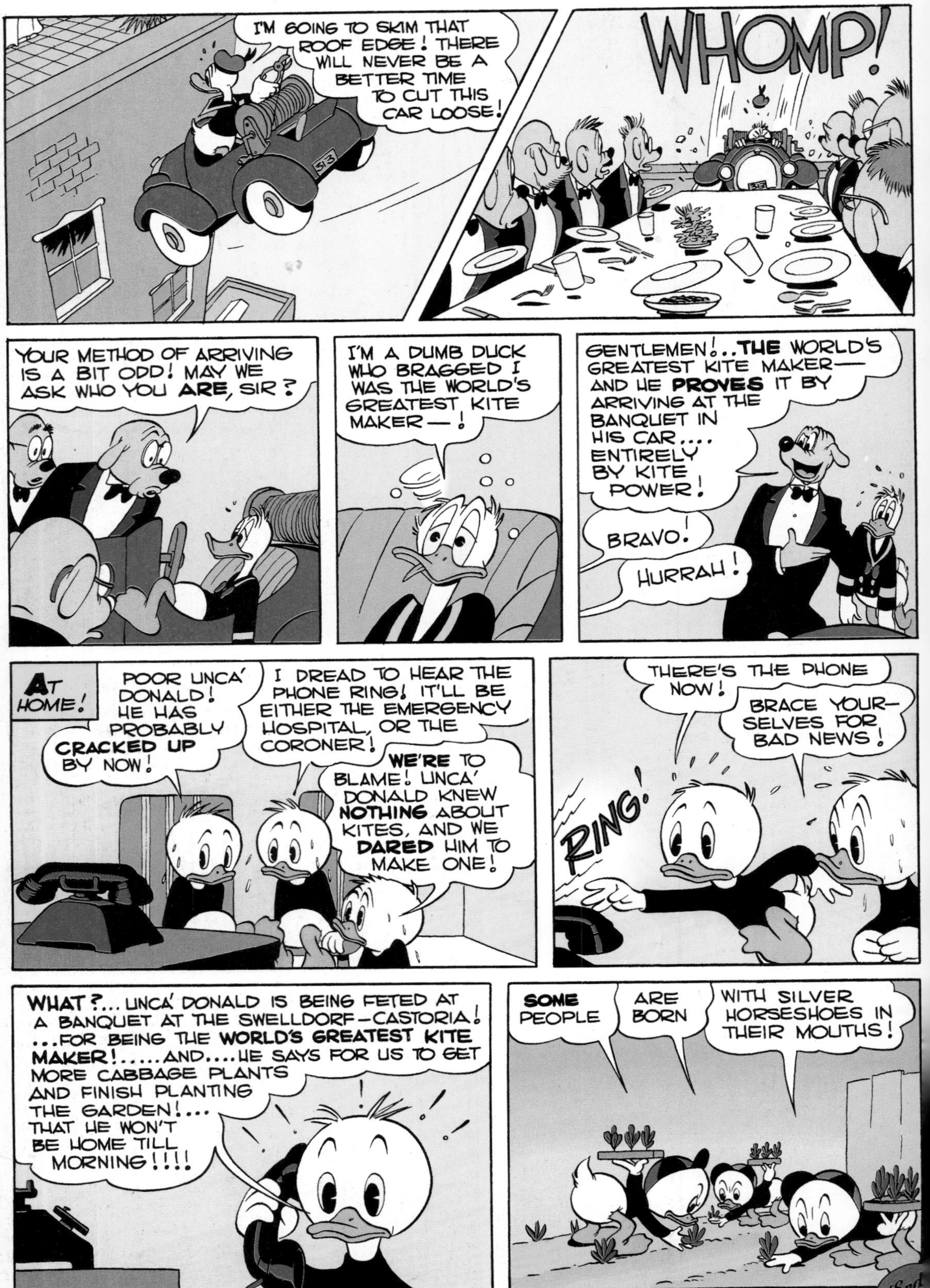

I'M GOING TO SKIM THAT ROOF EDGE! THERE WILL NEVER BE A BETTER TIME TO CUT THIS CAR LOOSE!
WHOMP!
YOUR METHOD OF ARRIVING IS A BIT ODD! MAY WE ASK WHO YOU ARE, SIR?
I'M A DUMB DUCK WHO BRAGGED I WAS THE WORLD'S GREATEST KITE MAKER—!
GENTLEMEN!..THE WORLD'S GREATEST KITE MAKER— AND HE PROVES IT BY ARRIVING AT THE BANQUET IN HIS CAR.... ENTIRELY BY KITE POWER!
BRAVO!
HURRAH!
AT HOME!
POOR UNCA' DONALD! HE HAS PROBABLY CRACKED UP BY NOW!
I DREAD TO HEAR THE PHONE RING! IT'LL BE EITHER THE EMERGENCY HOSPITAL, OR THE CORONER!
WE'RE TO BLAME! UNCA' DONALD KNEW NOTHING ABOUT KITES, AND WE DARED HIM TO MAKE ONE!
THERE'S THE PHONE NOW!
BRACE YOURSELVES FOR BAD NEWS!
RING!
WHAT?... UNCA' DONALD IS BEING FETED AT A BANQUET AT THE SWELLDORF-CASTORIA! ...FOR BEING THE WORLD'S GREATEST KITE MAKER!.....AND....HE SAYS FOR US TO GET MORE CABBAGE PLANTS AND FINISH PLANTING THE GARDEN!... THAT HE WON'T BE HOME TILL MORNING!!!!
SOME PEOPLE
ARE BORN
WITH SILVER HORSESHOES IN THEIR MOUTHS!
End